DEATH AT THE VILLAGE CHRISTMAS FAIR

DEBBIE YOUNG

Boldwood

First published in Great Britain in 2025 by Boldwood Books Ltd.

Copyright © Debbie Young, 2025

Cover Design by Lizzie Gardiner

Cover Images: Shutterstock and Adobe Stock

A CIP catalogue record for this book is available from the British Library.

Paperback ISBN 978-1-83518-582-7

Large Print ISBN 978-1-83518-583-4

Hardback ISBN 978-1-83518-581-0

Ebook ISBN 978-1-83518-584-1

Kindle ISBN 978-1-83518-585-8

Audio CD ISBN 978-1-83518-576-6

MP3 CD ISBN 978-1-83518-577-3

Digital audio download ISBN 978-1-83518-580-3

This book is printed on certified sustainable paper. Boldwood Books is dedicated to putting sustainability at the heart of our business. For more information please visit https://www.boldwoodbooks.com/about-us/sustainability/

Boldwood Books Ltd, 23 Bowerdean Street, London, SW6 3TN

www.boldwoodbooks.com

In fond memory of Mr & Mrs Kidd, the kindly proprietors of Rema's, the wool shop at The Oval, Sidcup, Kent

1

DEATH AT THE WOOL SHOP

'Good news, Alice,' said Mum. 'Old Mrs Hardy's dead.'

Even though I couldn't see Mum at the other end of the phone, I could tell from the warmth in her voice that she had a smile as broad as a Cheshire cat's.

'Mum! How can that possibly be good news?'

I was shocked by her uncharacteristic callousness. Mrs Hardy was the proprietor of The Woolgatherer, a mainstay of the shopping parade in the Norfolk market town where I grew up, and where Mum has lived alone since Dad died a few years ago.

Mum and I had been frequent visitors to The Woolgatherer, first for Mum to buy yarn for the jumpers and cardigans she knitted for me when I was little, and later for me to pursue my own craft projects. When I was about five, Mum taught me to knit on children's needles small enough for my tiny hands to control. Thus began a lifelong addiction, fed by frequent visits to The Woolgatherer and anywhere else that sold needlecraft materials.

Kind Mrs Hardy encouraged me by setting aside packs of yarn in her stock room, so that I'd have the same dye lot with which to complete my garment. (If you know, you know.) That meant I could buy the materials for expensive projects by instalments, as my pocket money permitted. I can still picture the first jumper I completed, in stripes of three garish shades of purple, my favourite colour at the time.

Since I'd left home and moved to the other side of the country, I used to call in to see Mrs Hardy whenever I was visiting my parents, and I always made a point of buying something from her shop, even if I didn't really need it. That's no great sacrifice for a dedicated knitter like me. I was flattered that Mrs Hardy always remembered me, even when she became so old and frail that she had to serve all her customers sitting down.

After Dad died, Mum began to visit The Woolgatherer more frequently, for company as much as for craft supplies. She started to cover for Mrs Hardy so that she didn't have to close the shop for her increasingly frequent hospital appointments. Mrs Hardy, also a widow, paid her in kind, which suited Mum, and they had become close friends. So, it was extremely odd that Mum seemed so jubilant at the poor old lady's demise.

'Let me explain,' she said. 'I hadn't told you how ill she was, because I didn't want you to worry.'

Perhaps that's where my own reticence comes from. Over the last few years, I'd drifted away from Mum. At the time, it seemed easier than telling her my twenty-five-year relationship with Steven was crumbling.

'You see, she'd become so unwell over the last year that I was holding the fort for her almost full-time. She was planning to retire, for the sake of her health, when the shop lease expires next June, and she'd been running down her stock. But, poor soul, the cancer had other plans. She was taken one evening in the flat above her shop as she sat quietly knitting another baby hat for the maternity hospital, listening to the radio. I found her the next day when I went to look for her, noticing she hadn't opened the shop. I had a spare latchkey, you see, so I could let myself in, in case of emergencies. Poor love, she looked so peaceful, and the little woolly hat was as neat as the ones she made before she was ill. I finished it off for her and took it to the hospital the next day. I knew she'd have wanted me to. And now she's free of pain and at peace at last. Her passing was a blessing after what she'd been through these last few months.'

'I wish you'd told me earlier that she was poorly,' I said, blinking back tears. 'I'd have sent her a get-well card.'

'It wouldn't have helped,' said Mum. 'She knew it was terminal.'

'Yes, but at least she'd have known I was thinking of her.'

'She'd rather you didn't. She didn't want people to know she was poorly. She was old-school like that.'

That was rich, coming from my seventy-five-year-old mother, keeper of secrets extraordinaire. Pot, kettle.

'So, when's the funeral? I'll close the shop for a few days and come across for it.'

'There won't be a funeral,' said Mum. 'She left her body to science, rather than have any fuss, bless her.'

Dear, kind Mrs Hardy. I decided at once to knit a floral wreath in her memory. I may have missed her non-funeral, but the wreath would be a lasting tribute to her in my little shop, marked *not for sale*, in all-year-round acceptable pastel colours.

'She's left all her remaining stock to me,' Mum continued. 'So, that's the good news.'

At last, she was making sense.

'Which means I can make loads of knitwear for you to sell in your shop, except now the materials won't cost us a penny.'

On Mum's first visit to my new home in Little Pride, I'd offered to take anything she cared to knit as stock for my

Cotswold Curiosity Shop, provided it matched the pretty, vintage vibe I was aiming for.

'So, what would you like me to make first?' Mum asked. 'Mrs Hardy had got in masses of pillar-box red and bright green, ready for Christmas. How about a nice supply of Christmas jumpers and Santa hats?'

'Great!' I said. 'I was looking for ways to make my shop look festive. I'm sure the elvish quarter of Little Pride will be thrilled.'

'Or how about some knitted holly wreaths or bunting?'

'That too,' I said, hoping I would have enough space to display them.

Then I remembered the advert for the village Christmas fair that I'd just been sent to include in the December issue of the *Little Pride Parish News*, of which I was now editor. I'd planned to book a stall, because the fair was raising funds for the village school library, but it seemed a bit pointless just shipping stock from my shop to the village hall. After all, villagers could browse my shop any time they liked in the run-up to Christmas. Now Mum had come up with a much better idea.

'I tell you what, make anything Christmassy that takes your fancy, and I'll hire a stall to sell it at the Christmas fair. You can fill it with your red and green creations, and it'll look fabulous.'

I didn't say, but I was glad of the excuse it would provide for Mum to visit again at the start of December, so that she could deliver her festive wares.

'By the way, if you need any buttons for any of your festive goods, wait until you get to mine. I've got tons of them. I've been buying up button boxes from elderly ladies in the village, and I've got enough buttons to last me a lifetime of crafting, and then some.'

It was true. On the counter in front of me were four big old toffee tins full of buttons. In a moment of impulsive generosity,

I'd paid over the odds for Maudie Frampton's collection, knowing how much the old lady needed the money. Getting wind of this, two other villagers had brought me theirs. I also had a huge box of the things left by my Curiosity Shop's previous owner, Nell Littlewood.

'I'm just sorting them out by colour and type, so I'll set aside any interesting novelty ones, and any in Christmassy colours, and you can sew them onto your finished garments when you get here. Now, when do you plan to visit? The fair's on the second Saturday in December.'

'Goodness! I'd better get busy. I'll look out my old book of fair knits too – tea cosies, socks and cuddly toys, and so forth.'

She sounded thrilled at her self-imposed challenge, and I was glad to be able to give her a new sense of purpose, now that she no longer had poor Mrs Hardy to help. I was also relieved to have found an outlet for at least a small quantity of the avalanche of buttons that had come into my possession.

2

FOR THE LOVE OF SMALL THINGS

After Mum rang off, I returned to my task of sorting the buttons. My initial task was clear: to separate functional, relatively modern buttons from fancier vintage ones. I was thinking of selling colour-themed bags of modern buttons as craft materials, while saving the more ornate ones for knitting projects, although where I'd find the time to knit enough garments to use up all these, I had no idea.

I don't usually pay villagers for the items they bring me to sell until I've actually sold them, but I did for the buttons, because the thought of trying to keep track of the sales of individual buttons was a non-starter. Instead, I'd paid a modest amount of cash up front for each tin.

The arrival of my friend Coralie, the village hairdresser, provided a welcome interruption. Coralie lived in an old shepherd's hut behind Coralie's Curls, her hairdressing salon housed in a small converted barn.

'Ah, buttons,' she breathed, eyes wide with excitement as she surveyed the counter.

'Afternoon, Cinders,' I quipped.

'That's a lot of buttons,' she said, dabbling her fingers into one of the tins to reveal what might lie beneath the top layer.

'Yes, and my quest is to turn them into gold. Or to sell them on, at least.'

She grinned as she set a wicker punnet of late raspberries on the counter, no doubt picked from the bountiful allotment she cultivated beside Coralie's Curls.

'Are you up for swapsies?' she asked, picking up a handful of unsorted buttons and turning them over in her palm. 'A button per berry?'

'Sure, but take as many as you like. I have more than I can possibly use.'

'I could make you some button necklaces and earrings to sell in your shop if you like, on the usual commission,' suggested Coralie.

I nodded. That line of crafts would fit in well with my shop, as did many of Coralie's crafts, which otherwise she displayed in her salon and online in her Etsy shop.

'Deal!'

When she gave me a double thumbs-up, I noticed how red her hands were from her raspberry picking. The berries must have been very ripe to yield their juice so easily this late in the season. The little punnet on my counter would probably be my last taste of them until the next summer.

'I just love buttons,' she continued. 'In fact, I adore any small items that I can repurpose into jewellery. Postage stamps. I love postage stamps too. They make great earrings. So, if you ever find yourself in possession of old stamp albums that you don't know what to do with, send them my way. Their scale suits my tiny house. But if I ever show signs of wanting to take up anything bulky like weaving, please stage an intervention to save me from myself.'

I truly admired Coralie's compact, minimalist lifestyle. I thought the cottage that came with my shop was small, but Coralie's home was more like a Wendy house than a home for a grown-up.

'Button jewellery goes down very well on my Etsy store,' she said. 'It's cheap and easy to post, which makes it relatively profitable. Although at the moment I'm stockpiling products for my stall at the Christmas fair.'

'I'm going to book a stall there too now,' I said. 'My mum's coming down at the start of December with a load of Christmas knits. The Little Pride Christmas Fair sounds the ideal outlet for them.'

'Good idea,' said Coralie, moving onto the next box and sifting its contents through her stained fingers, apparently enjoying the feel of the different materials and shapes. I hoped the dried raspberry juice on her hands wouldn't rub off on the buttons. 'The fair is always heaving with people, and not just the usual suspects from the village, because it takes place just after the Santa Run.'

'The Santa Run?' I echoed.

'Oh yes, don't you know about the Santa Run? I suppose not, as it'll be your first Christmas in Little Pride. It's been going for donkey's years, and people come from miles around to take part. It's a sight worth seeing, I can tell you. Anyone can take part, as long as they dress like Father Christmas. A small entry fee covers the cost of medals for completers, plus it pays for the cost of the Christmas tree on the village green. And the outsiders boost the fair's profits, especially the food and drink stalls.'

To my fellow villagers, anyone originating from beyond the *Welcome to* and *Leaving Little Pride* signs counted as outsiders, and their spend here as foreign currency.

I fished a few Bakelite buttons from a square shortbread tin and dropped them onto the counter. I'd recently heard of a Bakelite museum down in Somerset, and I wondered whether they might like these to add to their collection.

'That sounds like fun,' I said. 'I'm looking forward to spending my first Christmas here. Not that there weren't plenty of festive decorations and events in Broadwick, and we always put on a good show at Broadwick City Museum when I worked there. But I'm ready to embrace a village Christmas. I'm guessing it'll be a lot more traditional and less commercial than a city-centre one.'

Coralie wrinkled her nose. 'I wouldn't know, having never lived anywhere but here. But I do know I wouldn't miss a Little Pride Christmas for anything. So, does that mean you're definitely spending the Christmas holidays here? Not going home to your mum in Norfolk?'

I lowered my voice. 'To be honest, I was rather hoping Robert might invite me to spend Christmas Day with his family.'

Coralie raised her eyebrows. 'Going that well, is it, between you two? Best of luck to you. Old Bob Sponge must have been lonely since his wife died a few years ago, and it's about time he got back out there.'

'Less of the "old", thanks. He's only ten years older than me – just sixty. But yes, we've had a few dates now, mostly at his house or mine, but no less enjoyable for that.'

Nicknamed Bob Sponge by villagers for his invention of the everlasting washing-up sponge on which he'd built a lucrative global business, Robert's real surname was Praed. Just as well, as I didn't fancy the chance of ending up as Mrs A. Sponge. Not that I was thinking that far ahead. It was early days in our relationship, but after we'd worked together to solve a couple of local mysteries, we'd become quite close very quickly. A romantic Christmas with him wouldn't do either of us any harm.

I felt a pang of guilt at the thought of Mum being home alone over Christmas, especially now she'd lost her best friend, Mrs Hardy.

'Actually, I think I'll ask Mum to stay on after the fair to spend Christmas here too.'

Coralie's face lit up like a – no, I won't say it. 'Good call, Alice. What a good daughter you are. She'll love a Little Pride Christmas too. I'm sure you won't regret it.'

I hoped she was right.

3

THE BAD PENNY

Engrossed in sorting the remaining buttons after Coralie had taken what she wanted, I didn't notice the shop door open and a new visitor enter until a pair of hairy hands thumped down on the sales counter in front of me.

'How are the mighty fallen.'

The deep, familiar voice immediately grated on my nerves.

I looked up to see Martin, the ex-boyfriend of my lodger Danny, and a former colleague to both of us at Broadwick City Museum. Martin had moved away from Broadwick after falling under suspicion of spiking my drink in the pub where we were mourning the redundancy of several workers, myself included.

Danny had immediately fled Martin's flat, where he'd been living, and he'd moved into my spare bedroom to give him time to find a new place of his own. He'd been lodging with me ever since.

Having assumed both of us had seen the last of Martin, I was astonished by his nerve in waltzing into my shop now, with his usual condescending attitude.

How I wished I could have proven Martin's guilt! It might have stopped him from ever repeating his ghastly crime. Unfortunately, no one had spotted him in the act, and the effect the drugs had on me were at first mistaken by traffic police for alcohol abuse, so they didn't press charges on Martin. But Danny and I knew the truth, and Martin knew that we knew. I'd hoped his narrow escape from a career-ending conviction would make him keep his distance from Danny and me forever.

'What do you mean?' I retorted.

He'd only been in my shop for a moment, and already he was winding me up. He nodded at the array of buttons on the counter.

'Do buttons count as cash around these parts? Is this how the local yokels pay you?'

Ignoring my half-sorted piles, I scooped the loose buttons back into the tins, wanting to protect my little treasures from the tarnish of Martin's insults.

'I was paid buttons at Broadwick City Museum, as you well know,' I replied tersely. 'Being made redundant was the best thing that ever happened to me. Now I'm my own boss, and I call the shots. I don't have to put up with any nonsense from unpleasant colleagues.'

I hoped my hard stare might cause him to turn on his heel and leave. Instead, he leaned forward over the counter, as if hoping to intimidate me with his superior height.

'Unpleasant colleagues? Surely you don't mean me?'

His question didn't deserve an answer. I turned away, pretending to busy myself with some papers under the till.

'Danny told me you'd left Broadwick City Museum,' I said, hoping that might give me the upper hand. 'Or did they sack you?'

'I left of my own accord, actually, to start a job I'd been offered before you were made redundant. A much better job, as it happens, at a much better museum.'

I could tell he was just dying for me to ask him about his new job so that he could show off about it, but I wasn't going to give him that pleasure.

'So have you come to my shop just to gloat?' I asked. 'Or do you want to buy something?'

Martin peered over my shoulder towards the open door that led to my living accommodation.

'Actually, I was rather hoping to see Danny,' he admitted. 'When I phoned to speak to him at Broadwick City Museum today, they told me he was on a day off. The fool of a human resources officer gave me his new home address when I asked for it. So much for confidentiality. So' – he spread his arms as if claiming territory – 'here I am.'

The museum's human resources officer was not as daft as Martin thought. She may have slipped up by letting out Danny's new home address, but he was very much not having a day off today. She was just fobbing Martin off to protect Danny.

Martin plunged his hands into two of my button boxes, his stocky fingers displacing enough of them to make the sea of tiny discs spill over the rims of the toffee tins. Without thinking, I slapped his wrist, feeling his gesture as an assault on my private space.

'Oi, paws off!' I commanded.

To my relief and surprise, he withdrew his fingers immediately and slid his hands nonchalantly into the front pockets of his close-fitting khaki jeans, set off by an immaculate conker-brown Gucci belt. With his rugged Icelandic jumper and his soft leather brogues, he looked as dapper as ever. Danny, I thought with regret, would be impressed. Perhaps Martin had made a special effort with his appearance today for Danny's sake.

'I'm afraid she's sent you on a wild goose chase.' I forced myself to look away from the enviable hand-knitted sweater – at least a couple of hundred quid's worth, and built to withstand a Nordic winter. 'Danny's not here, and even if he was, I doubt he'd want to see you. If you've something to say to him, why don't you just email him?'

This was a safe option, because I knew that Danny, keen to draw a line under their relationship, especially now that he was in a promising new romance with local schoolteacher Jack Dauntless, had blocked Martin online, both from his work and personal email accounts and from his phone and social media. By now, I felt I had the upper hand, and I was enjoying it.

'Now, Martin, if you're not planning to buy anything, I'd thank you to leave my shop.'

The sound of the shop door opening alerted me to the arrival of my kind and charming next-door neighbour, Robert Praed, clutching the hand of his spirited seven-year-old granddaughter, Tilly.

'So that I can attend to proper customers,' I added, hoping that Robert wouldn't give the game away by greeting me with a kiss. Danny was not the only one enjoying a new romance.

Although it was early days, things were going so well with Robert, a widower, that to my embarrassment – OK, also to my delight – Tilly was already rooting for me to become her new grandmother.

I shot a frantic look at Robert, trying to communicate by cryptic eye movements that I would welcome his intervention. A perceptive soul, Robert gave me the slightest of nods behind Martin's back.

Martin took a couple of steps back from the counter, looked

Robert up and down, and heaved an exaggerated sigh of frustration.

'OK, perhaps I'll catch Danny another time,' he said. 'Thanks for nothing.'

Without more ado, he marched to the shop door and let himself out, slamming it behind him like a sulky teenager.

4

THE GOOD OMEN

Robert raised his eyebrows at me. 'Awkward customer?'

'You could put it that way. Anyway, best forgotten. How are you two? Good day at school, Tilly?'

'Always,' said Tilly smoothly. A natural optimist, she didn't let much get her down. She stood on tiptoe to peer inside the button boxes on the counter. 'Those look interesting, Alice. Please may I play with them?'

'They're not toys, Tilly,' said Robert quickly, but I swiftly over-ruled him. What small child wouldn't enjoy playing with a tin of assorted buttons of all shapes, sizes and designs? I knew I did at Tilly's age, inventing countless games with them. I could still picture the red and gold sweet tin my grandma kept her buttons in, and I remembered my favourites among her buttons – little silver daisies and tiny pink mice.

I passed a tin down to Tilly and pointed to one of the tea tables inside the shop. Now that it was November, chilly, grey and damp, I'd brought a couple of the tables from the front patio indoors, moving some of my display closer together to make a space. Serving refreshments added a useful boost to the shop's takings most days, and I didn't want to lose that income stream during the winter months.

One small hand already rummaging through the tin's contents, Tilly made her way to an empty table and sat down. Robert lingered to chat to me at the counter while I made his usual cappuccino and poured Tilly an elderflower cordial.

'So, what's new in Alice's Cotswold Curiosity Shop today?' he asked, idly stirring a tin of buttons with one forefinger, making a pleasing rattling sound. Whatever your age, there is something irresistible about buttons. The urban myth about a hundred kinds of germs (or worse) populating a bar-room bowl of peanuts sprang to mind. At this rate, what with Coralie, Martin, Tilly and Robert all fingering them, I'd have to sterilise all the buttons before I could sell them.

'Nothing's new in my shop, but I do have other news,' I replied. 'Mum's going to be heading this way again soon with a carload of her handknits. You know we agreed I'd sell her hand-knits in my shop when she was staying with me last month?'

Robert smiled fondly. That had been his first encounter with Mum, and, to my relief, given Mum and Dad had once rooted for my ex, Steven, they'd rather got on.

'Well, now she's inherited the stock of her local wool shop, there'll be no holding her back. You name it, she'll knit it – and bring it to sell in my shop.'

'That's handy,' he said brightly. He produced a folded slip of paper from his pocket and spread it out on the counter. 'Tilly's just been sent home from school with a request to rustle up an elf costume in time for the Christmas fair. Do you think Wendy could conjure up something suitable with her needles? I'd pay her for her time and materials, obviously.'

'Oh, she doesn't need any encouragement or payment,' I replied. 'She adores Tilly. I'm sure she'd be happy to knit a little elven tunic, cap and stripy leggings. All in a festive red and green, of course. Consider it an early Christmas present.'

Although Tilly attended our village school, she and her mother, Belinda, lived a couple of miles away in the much posher village of Great Pride.

'Magic,' said Robert. 'That'll get Belinda off the hook. Despite her interest in high fashion, she's strangely averse to conjuring up fancy-dress outfits for school.'

I'd been getting to know Belinda better lately, and I could tell she was not the sort to sit by the fire of an evening knitting elf costumes.

I set Robert's coffee on the counter and sprinkled it with cocoa powder through a stencil with a cut-out shaped like a snowflake. I looked at him coyly from beneath my eyelashes. 'Are you sure I can't tempt you to a matching outfit for her grandpa?'

He grinned. 'I'm already otherwise sorted, I'm afraid. Somehow, I've been volunteered to play Santa at the Christmas fair again. I get to dish out presents to the children who come to visit me in my grotto. The costume is provided as a perk of the job.'

I gave a surreptitious nod towards Tilly and lowered my voice to a whisper. 'Don't you think a certain little girl might rumble your disguise? Or does she still believe?'

He replied in similar confidential tones. 'Oh no, she believes all right. But all the village kids take me as Santa in their stride, on the basis that the real one will be too busy to swing by Little Pride so close to Christmas, centre of the universe though it is. Plus, of course, there'll be another couple of hundred Santas in the village that day. Not even the most gullible child would think any of us were the real thing.'

I smiled. 'Coralie's just been telling me about the Santa Run. Will you be taking part in the run too, as you'll have all the gear for it?'

Leaning one elbow on the counter, Robert picked up the spoon from his coffee saucer and idly traced the six points of the cocoa snowflake, blurring them into the foamy milk. 'No, I'll be saving my strength for my duties in my grotto. Now, I'd better take Tilly her cordial, or I'll be in trouble. Fancy a drink at mine later? About eight?'

'Love to,' I said. 'And then you can tell me more about the Little Pride Christmas.'

'I'll show you too, when the time comes,' he said with a wink, before turning his attention to his granddaughter.

For the first time in years, I was really looking forward to the festive season. Somehow, I already knew that my first Christmas in Little Pride would be like no other I'd ever experienced.

5

HOW NOT TO LEARN CHESS

I was glad Robert hadn't seen the *Chess for Simpletons* book I'd been reading before I'd spread the buttons all over the shop counter. It was only a matter of time before he invited me to a game of chess with the beautiful Alice in Wonderland set he'd bought, ostensibly for Tilly, at the sale of Steven's collectible chess sets I'd organised the previous month. Before Robert had even got the set home, Tilly, as keen on my growing relationship with him as Mum was, had suggested he and I play against each other sometimes. Due to Robert's status as a well-known, wealthy industrialist, he preferred date nights at home rather than going out. He wasn't keen on being spotted by the press going about his personal life in public. Paparazzi photos of him in a commercial context might serve as useful publicity for his business empire, but being papped on dates served no purpose that interested him.

So, in every spare moment, I was, in theory, swotting up on the rules of the game. Or, at least, picking up the how-to book and putting it down again. My intentions were of the best, my execution less so. I've always preferred productive hobbies that reward your efforts with something tangible and lasting, such as knitting or crochet. Conversely, with board games and jigsaw puzzles, as soon as you finish, you dismantle the results, leaving no trace of the time, effort and energy expended. It's as if those hours of your life have never existed.

Still, if playing chess would strengthen my romance with Robert, learning the rules was a sacrifice I was prepared to make. Both of us were cautious after the end of long-term relationships that had endured for almost all of our adult lives. Robert's long marriage ended in widowhood when Tilly was a baby. My twenty-five-year partnership was curtailed when Steven left me earlier in the year, determined to spend the rest of his life travelling, starting with a motorbike trip to India. It felt like it wasn't just me he was abandoning, but our whole lifestyle and our shared past.

It was a tough and thorough rejection, yet since my move to the surprisingly busy village of Little Pride, events had helped me move on – not least my burgeoning friendship with the dashing boy next door. OK, sixty-year-old man next door.

After turning the shop door sign to *Closed*, I'd just settled into the armchair in my little sitting room with the chess book in my hands when Danny arrived home from work.

'You're early,' I said as he slipped off his puffer jacket. 'Is everything OK?'

He glanced at his watch. 'No, I'm not.' He frowned in puzzlement. 'Early, that is. It's gone six.'

I glanced down at the chess book, which had slipped out of my grasp and now lay on the floor.

'Oops, I must have nodded off.' I gave an embarrassed grin at my lethargy. After all, Danny had a gruelling daily commute by car into Broadwick. I had only to walk from the sitting room to the shop.

I stooped to pick up off the floor a circular that I'd been using as a bookmark and slipped it between the pages of the book.

'But in answer to your second question,' he continued, 'no, everything isn't OK. There are rumours of further redundancies at the museum before Christmas. They're not replacing Martin, either.'

From his anxious expression, I guessed he thought he might be next for the chop. He slumped down on the sofa beside me.

'What am I meant to do? There are no other museums in Broadwick. I'll have to look further afield for a new job. But where? And there's no point in going ahead with my flat-hunting in Broadwick if I'm likely to get bounced out of my job the minute I move in.'

He lowered his head into his hands. 'I'm sorry, Alice, I know I was meant to be only a temporary lodger here. I promise I'll move on before I outstay my welcome – if I haven't already.'

I edged closer to him and laid a comforting arm around his hunched shoulders.

'Stay as long as you like,' I said, meaning it. It would have been handy to have the spare bedroom back for Mum, so I didn't have to give her my room and sleep on the sofa when she stayed, but I didn't really mind. She was worth it, and so was he.

'I have been keeping an eye out for other jobs,' said Danny, staring unseeingly into the fireplace. 'In case I get made redundant. I just hope I don't have to move too far away.'

'Of course not, now there's Jack to consider.'

Jack was a far more suitable match for Danny than Martin – kind, dependable and his intellectual equal. I'd been hoping Jack might prove The One for Danny, and not only to spite Martin.

Danny hauled himself up off the sofa and gave a big stretch, which must have released a little of his tension. When he reached up, his fingertips touched the low ceiling. People were much shorter when my Victorian cottage was built.

'It does no harm to look for other jobs,' I assured him. 'In fact, it can only help. But I'm not going to force your hand.'

6

A QUEST FOR BUTTONS

The next afternoon, just as I was thinking I never wanted to see another button again, a stranger in a beige gabardine raincoat and shiny brogues surprised me with his request.

'Buttons,' he said as he approached the counter. 'I'm after vintage buttons. Can I see your stock? I'm told you've plenty of them, and some fine examples too.'

I lifted the flap in the counter and came out from behind it to lead him across the shop floor to a small display of interesting craft materials. From the muddle Nell Littlewood had left when she moved out of the shop and into the old people's home at Wendlebury Barrow, I'd curated a pretty display of needlecraft paraphernalia and vintage knitting patterns, the kind sought by collectors for the comical poses of mid-century models. Matching pairs of steel and wooden knitting needles were tied with mauve ricrac braid. Cellophane envelopes of sets of buttons filled a wide green pressed-glass bowl with a riot of colour. From old floral fabric remnants, I'd assembled sets of fat quarters, the squares beloved by patchwork enthusiasts.

Ignoring my rainbow display of yarns and threads, the

stranger made straight for the bowl of buttons, plunging his hands in and stirring them up as if he knew exactly what he was looking for. I was glad I'd gone to the trouble of bagging them up in cellophane envelopes the previous evening.

'These aren't quite what I'm after,' he concluded after a minute of scrabbling about. 'They're all a bit flat.'

I blinked at him. 'Isn't that the general nature of buttons?'

He peered into the bowl. Many of the buttons bore raised patterns or trims, and some had metal loops at the back rather than holes through their centre.

'Not if they're toggles,' he replied.

'Oh, is it toggles you're after? Like the ones on Paddington Bear's duffel coat?'

Coralie had pounced on all the leather-effect toggles in my button tins, declaring they'd make perfect fasteners for her patchwork bags and cushions.

He considered for a moment. His tailored raincoat suggested he wasn't a duffel coat man. 'Yes, I suppose you could put them on duffel coats.'

I remained silent, hoping he might elaborate. But he didn't rise to my bait, staring dully at the green pressed-glass bowl. Beginning to feel sorry for disappointing him, I tried to help.

'Actually, I did have some toggles in stock, but I gave them to a friend who makes jewellery.'

He brightened. 'Is your friend local? Could I please have his or her address? I'd love to see them.'

He didn't look like a jewellery buff, his neat hands unadorned by rings, no visible piercings, a classic Swiss Railway watch his only adornment.

I looked him up and down. There was something about him that made me uneasy. Perhaps it was that he had dressed like a cartoon spy? He even had a furled copy of the *Daily Telegraph* under his arm. I wondered whether, if he opened it up, there'd be holes cut in the pages for his eyes. I decided not to tell him where Coralie lived.

'She has an Etsy shop,' I said. 'You could try there. I can give you its web address.'

'If that's the best you can do.'

His surly attitude made me all the more determined to safeguard Coralie from him.

In any case, I would never have directed a stranger to her secluded tiny house, hidden from passers-by by the small barn conversion housing her hairdressing salon, Coralie's Curls. At least my shop had big windows at the front, making the interior visible to passers-by. If a customer ever got out of hand, all I needed to do was signal my alarm to a dogwalker or school-run parent, and they'd come to my rescue. If Coralie had a troublesome visitor, passing pedestrians would be oblivious.

I took my purse out of my handbag, which I kept out of sight under the counter, and produced Coralie's business card for her Etsy shop. He pulled a mobile phone from his raincoat pocket to photograph the card, then marched out of the shop without so much as a thank you.

'Toggles to you too,' I hissed at the back of his raincoat as he strode across the terrace towards the pavement. Then I returned my attention to my bowl of buttons, rearranging them so that the most expensive packets, containing tiny mother-of-pearl flowers on exquisite silver filigree discs, were on the top.

7

BUTTONHOLED

The following week, between the school run and my usual opening time of 10 a.m., I took the opportunity to stroll up the empty high street to Suki's Stores for a quick grocery top-up shop. I was expecting a minibus of Japanese tourists for morning coffee at eleven, and I wanted to have plenty of refreshments at the ready. The more I fed them, the longer they'd linger, and the more they'd buy. I also had to make sure I had their driver's favourite lemon drizzle cake available – my part of the deal I'd made with Jim Hazletine, who hired himself and his vehicle out to tourists for Cotswold shopping trips.

To my surprise, Suki, not usually the chattiest of customer service operatives, couldn't wait to talk to me. I hadn't even closed her shop door before she leaned across the counter, eyes gleaming, to share the latest gossip.

'Did you hear about Coralie's break-in last night?' she whispered, as if she thought the culprits might be lurking behind the biscuit counter, and she didn't want them to overhear her.

'Oh, no! Is she OK?'

Suki dismissed my concern with a wave of her hand, long magenta nails glinting in the glare of the shop's fluorescent strip light. 'Coralie's fine. She was with me in The Quarrymen's Arms at the time, playing skittles. But when she got home, her tiny house was a tip. Buttons everywhere!'

I closed my eyes as I pictured the scene. How upsetting to have a stranger violate your personal space like that. 'It must have been tricky tidying up that lot after dark.'

Although Coralie's salon has an electricity supply, her tiny house is lit only by candles and oil lamps, and she cooks on a camping gas stove. In my view, the whole set-up is a fire waiting to happen, but that wasn't my biggest worry about her today.

'I hope she didn't disturb anything before calling the police.'

I wished she'd also called me. Coralie had been a good friend since I'd moved to Little Pride the previous summer, and I'd have been glad to support her for a change.

Suki shook her head. 'Nah. She checked her valuables, whatever they are, and didn't think anything had actually been stolen. No point in getting the cops involved. She reckoned it was probably just kids messing about, most likely some disgruntled youth seeking revenge for a haircut his mother forced upon him at Coralie's hands. She didn't want to make a big issue of it, especially if it meant getting a local lad into trouble.'

I set my wicker basket on the counter and fetched a couple of loaf cakes from the bakery section. 'That's very generous of her.' I wondered whether I'd be as forgiving in the circumstances. 'Was she OK to stay there alone last night after it happened? If I were her, I'd have wanted company. If I'd known, I would have invited her to my place.'

'Not Coralie.' Suki began to ring up my purchases as I added a packet of loose tea to my basket. I didn't want to risk insulting my Japanese visitors by giving them teabags, when I'd heard they took so much trouble with their own tea ceremony at home.

'Coralie's view was that whoever the culprit was wouldn't dare come back while she was at home. Besides, even if they did, she knows every kid in the village, where they live and who their parents are, so she could rat on them to their families. No, she was just going to tidy up and forget about it. Sometimes village kids do stuff like that when they're bored, just for the hell of it. I reckon the best way to put an end to their antics is to completely ignore what they've done.'

I wondered whether she was thinking back to her own youth. Like Coralie, she'd been born and raised in Little Pride.

'That certainly worked the time a kid graffitied the front of my Stores with some spray paint,' she continued. 'All I did was correct their spelling and let it sit there for a while. Actually, they did me a favour. A lot of locals who don't use the shop much came in especially to the get the low-down about this act of vandalism, under the guise of offering their condolences. Of course, they couldn't decently leave without buying something. My takings trebled that week.'

I smiled.

'With any luck, Coralie will get some sympathy haircuts out of it,' I speculated. 'And she might sell more than usual of the crafts she displays in her salon to anyone who doesn't need a haircut.'

'Like Samson Taylor,' said Suki, using the nickname of an elderly villager whose scalp was as bald as a boulder.

I glanced at the clock above the shelf of spirits, which bore the slogan *Wine O'Clock* at all times of day. It was 9.15 a.m. – still plenty of time before I opened my shop.

'I think I'll pop round to see Coralie on my way home, just to make sure she's not suffering from delayed shock.'

That was my excuse, anyway. Perhaps I was just as bad as everyone else in the village, wanting to hear the gossip at first hand.

8

AN AWKWARD MOMENT

'Coralie, it's only me,' I shouted at the foot of the wooden steps to her tiny house. Her salon, which stood on the same plot of land but closer to the pavement, still had the *Closed* sign on the door, so I assumed she'd still be in her shepherd's hut.

In response to my call, the upper half of the stable-style door to the hut flew open, and Coralie leaned out, one clenched fist raised. Startled, I took a step back.

'What kind of a welcome is that?'

Coralie looked down at her fist and laughed. 'Don't worry, I wasn't about to punch you.'

Turning her hand palm upward, she spread her fingers to reveal a handful of buttons. 'I'm just gathering up all the buttons some wretched tearaway scattered all over my floor while I was at the pub last night.'

With her free hand, she unbolted the lower half of the door and beckoned me to clamber up the steps to join her inside.

'Just tread carefully,' she warned me. 'I'm still in tidy-up mode here. I can tell you now, the pain of treading on one of the chunkier buttons in bare feet is second only to the agony of stepping on Lego, especially the type with little metal loops at the back.'

For emphasis, she balanced on one leg and shook her raised foot.

Setting my shopping basket on the step behind me, I entered the hut, tiptoeing around the tiny obstacles scattered across the narrow aisle.

'Shepherd's huts aren't really built for more than one, are they?' I observed as I squeezed past her and hopped up onto the only part of the bench seat that wasn't covered in button boxes, fabric and other craft materials. I eased off my shoes so that I could raise my feet onto the bench without soiling the pretty sky-blue gingham fabric.

'Let me help you,' I offered, bending double to pick up buttons without leaving my seat. 'It's the least I can do since I got you into this mess.'

Coralie stood still for a moment, staring at me.

'What do you mean? Just because some little toad scattered the buttons you kindly gave me doesn't make it your fault. If I hadn't left the button boxes out, they'd have seized whatever else came to hand, like my tin of pins, or the cutlery drawer. Serves me right for breaking the first rule of tiny house living: always put everything away once you've finished with it. You'd think I'd know that by now. I just thank goodness this wasn't one of my weeks for dying, is all I can say.'

I drew back in horror, banging my head on the pale green wooden wall panel behind me. 'Dying? Oh, Coralie, don't say that! I know some of the local children can be a bit mischievous, but surely you don't think any of them are capable of murder?'

With a roar of laughter, Coralie threw herself down on the bench seat opposite me, on top of a pile of fabric.

'Not that sort of dying, silly.' She dropped her handful of

buttons into an empty tin. "'Dyeing" with an "e" in it – dyeing fabric and wool.'

I huffed a sigh of relief as I rubbed the back of my head. 'Sorry! I didn't mean to catastrophise, but you had me worried for a moment.'

She reached across to light the gas burner beneath her kettle. 'Got time for a cup of tea before you open your Curiosity Shop? I was just going to have one.'

I nodded. 'Tea cures all.'

She lifted a pair of mugs down from Shaker hooks above the stove. As she plucked a handful of fresh herbs from a water-filled jam jar and dropped them into the chocolate-brown stoneware teapot, my smile faded.

'Actually, I might be slightly responsible for what happened here,' I began. 'You see, I'm thinking that the culprit isn't some local kid, but a peculiar man who came into my shop last week in search of toggles.'

Coralie took a teaspoon from the cutlery drawer and tapped it thoughtfully against her open palm. 'Toggles? Are you sure that's not code for some kind of illicit drug? Maybe he'd mistaken your quirky shop for an undercover dealer.'

That thought had never crossed my mind. Was there something Nell Littlewood hadn't told me about her trading days? I'd already discovered from my visits to her with Robert, who had known her since he was a little boy, that there was more to the old lady than met the eye, but I wouldn't have put her down as a drug pusher. It just goes to show that you should never underestimate the elderly. They were all young once, and you never knew what their back story might be. Then I remembered a vital detail of my conversation with the stranger.

'No, he did specify that he meant the sort of toggle you find on duffel coats.'

Coralie nodded sagely. 'Like that global style icon, Paddington Bear.'

'My thoughts exactly.' I laughed. 'Which surprised me, really, as my visitor didn't look the duffel coat type – more the Burberry brigade. If he'd come in dressed like Paddington, I'd have warmed to him straight away. As it was, he just gave me the creeps, though I can't put my finger on why.'

'Enough for you to think he'd stage a raid on my house for toggles? Nonsense, Alice! As he wasn't a local, how would he even know I had any? It's not as if I advertise my crafts on the side of my hut. I know I showcase some of my stuff inside the salon, but I've not had anyone matching your man's description coming into my salon for a haircut lately. Or ever, come to think of it. Local folk don't go in for Burberry macs; they're not very practical in the countryside. They show the dirt.'

I gazed out of the little window at her vegetable plot. I was too ashamed to look her in the eye as I made my confession.

'Actually, I told him about your Etsy store.'

Coralie raised the boiling kettle to fill the teapot. 'So what? It's not like you painted a big target on the side of my tiny house.'

Coralie picked up the teapot and swirled it around to speed up the brewing process.

'I'd never have sent him here in person. I honestly thought he might buy some of your button jewellery online. From his smart dress, he looked like a middle-class family man who might have a wife or daughter at home.'

'Alice, stop worrying! You're letting your imagination run away with you. I'm sure it's just the work of some pesky local kid. My money's on Ethan Timms. He's got form, you know. Last time I cut his hair, he pulled up a row of radishes from my allotment the minute he was out of the salon. I told his mum yesterday I'm never cutting his hair again. She can do it herself in future. That'll teach him.'

When she handed me my mug of herbal tea, it felt like a peace offering. I was glad when she changed the subject to her plans for the imminent Christmas fair instead.

Even so, as soon as I returned to my shop, I wrote down as detailed a description of the stranger as I could remember, in case it was ever needed. Then I tucked it away in my desk and pledged to forget about it, before opening my shop for the day.

9

A PRIVATE SUPPER

By the time November had segued into December, with fairy lights popping up in front gardens and holly wreaths appearing on front doors, there were no further developments on the ransacking of Coralie's tiny house. I was increasingly inclined to believe her theory that some local youth was responsible, although their attack seemed most uncalled for.

'I don't see how a local kid could be so mean to Coralie,' I said to Robert on the Saturday evening as we shared a lasagna in his spacious kitchen.

I was giving Danny my cottage to himself for the evening so that he could invite Jack Dauntless to supper, an overdue return of many such evenings he'd spent at Jack's flat a few miles away. Like most schoolteachers, Jack preferred not to live too close to his place of work for fear of bumping into his pupils off duty.

I was doing all I could to nurture their relationship without being obvious. Danny deserved a bit of luck in love after the fiasco with Martin. I'd even picked fresh flowers from the garden for the kitchen table. The last few roses soldiering on since summer added a romantic touch. Perhaps the less charitable part of me also secretly welcomed an opportunity for subtle revenge against Martin.

'Maybe the kids were just bored,' said Robert, spooning a generous helping of lasagna onto my plate. 'There's not a lot for teenagers to do around here in winter, when it's too cold and wet to play ball games on the rec or to cycle around the lanes. Besides, most kids must be curious to see the inside of Coralie's tiny house. From the outside it looks very like a playhouse. Few people have ever been inside it, as far as I know.'

Certainly, after all the times Coralie had visited my shop and dropped into my cottage for coffee and a chat, she'd never invited me back to hers. I helped myself to a small heap of gleaming green leaves from the crystal salad bowl.

'Then I'm honoured,' I replied. 'The other day, she invited me inside for the first time.'

I toyed with the stem of my glass, gazing at the rich ruby wine. 'Actually, she didn't so much invite me, as let me invade her territory. I called on her unannounced after Suki had told me about her break-in. Do you think I overstepped the mark? I'd hate her to feel I was invading her privacy just as the house-breakers did. I may have lived in Little Pride for six months now, but sometimes I still feel as if I'm struggling to find my way around the local etiquette.'

Robert reached across the table to lay a reassuring hand on mine. 'Don't worry, Coralie is sufficiently assertive that she wouldn't have let you in if she didn't want to – although the unpleasant circumstances may have weakened her resolve. Anyway, once you've been in Little Pride a year and lived through all the seasons, it won't all seem so alien. Just hang in there.'

Robert always knew the right thing to say to make me feel better. He took his hand away from mine to raise his glass to me. 'Here's to your first Little Pride Christmas.'

With a smile, I clinked my glass against his before taking a sip of the spicy liquid, thinking of the romantic winter evenings that lay ahead, drinking mulled wine together by our firesides.

'Maybe what I need is for someone entirely new to move to the village so that I'm no longer the new kid on the block,' I suggested. 'I don't think I've seen a single "for sale" sign go up here since mine came down.'

'That's just NULPY,' replied Robert.

At least I'd been there long enough to know that NULPY meant Not Unusual for Little Pride. Being able now to translate some of the local shorthand gave me a pleasant frisson of belonging.

'Maybe what we need is some nice new-builds to bring in a crowd of townies.' Robert's face and voice were deadpan, but the twinkle in his dark eyes told me he was teasing.

When I first moved in, I discovered to my horror a plan to fill the old meadow next to my house with tacky executive homes. The project fell apart when the builder ended up in prison before getting beyond the foundations, but that's another story.

'Speaking of the abandoned plot, I wonder what's going to happen to it now.'

I hoped another dodgy builder wouldn't take over the site and complete the project. I still mourned the absence of the donkeys who had grazed there when I first viewed the Curiosity Shop with the ill-informed estate agent. My grief was slightly relieved by the knowledge that Robert had bought the donkeys before the building project started. He'd rehomed them in one of the farms that he owns across the Cotswolds. With a modest lifestyle but a huge income, Robert had been spending his surplus in saving and restoring derelict or failing farms across the Cotswolds and renting them out. To me, that made him much more lovable than if he'd been splashing out on private jets or luxury yachts, which I suspect his income would have run to. Farms must have been a more future-proof investment too. Who was it who advised his son to 'invest in land, my boy – they're not making any more of it'?

Robert leaned over the table confidentially. 'Don't put this in the *Parish News* yet, but I hear the council's entertaining a bid from a private investor. Doubtless they'll require any buyer to remove the ill-fated foundations and clear all evidence of the failed building site, as well as to preserve the Roman remains that lie beneath.'

Robert and I had been instrumental in discovering a complete mosaic floor under the site, a remnant of the small villa built in the era when the village was just a hamlet named Praeda Parva.

'With any luck, they'll return the land to pasture out of the goodness of their hearts,' I surmised. 'It's perfectly acceptable to rebury Roman mosaics to preserve their integrity ad infinitum. There's no obligation to turn them into museums, unfortunately. As I know only too well, trying to keep existing museums open and solvent is hard enough, never mind building a whole new one. By the way, did I tell you Danny's job-hunting now? He's fearful of redundancy. Broadwick City Museum might even close down.'

Robert finished chewing a forkful of lasagna before he replied. 'I doubt the council would let Broadwick City Museum close altogether. Surely just reducing staff would resolve the situation? Or they could start charging entry fees. Closure would lay the council open to all sorts of accusations about destroying local heritage and devaluing the town as a tourist attraction.'

'You're right. Still, I hope Danny will be OK. He'll probably have to move away to wherever he can get a new job. I'll miss him, of course, but his departure wouldn't be disastrous for me.

I'm making enough from the shop now that I don't need his rent to pay my bills. Plus it would free up my spare room for visitors like my mum.'

Robert concentrated on topping up our glasses for a moment. 'Fingers crossed that the right job turns up on his doorstep before too long. Anyway, speaking of your mum, when is Wendy coming to stay again?'

'Next weekend. And don't worry, she's already finished Tilly's elf outfit, as well as knitting enough stuff to fill a whole stall at the Christmas fair.'

I pulled my phone from my skirt pocket and summoned up the slightly blurry shot that Mum had sent me the night before. When I showed it to Robert, he smiled his approval.

'Tilly will love it. I bet your mum will be in her element at the fair. It's one of the highlights of the village year, even for me after all the dozens of times I have attended. I confess I always make sure I'm never away on business at fair time so I don't miss it. Does that make me a big kid?'

I laughed. 'Not at all. After all, you are the star of the show, playing Santa.'

He nudged my calf with the soft toe of one of his mauve merino socks. 'I just hope you've been a good girl this year so Santa can bring you something nice.'

I raised my glass to him as I pondered his remark. What on earth was I to buy Robert for Christmas? Here was a man wealthy enough to buy whatever he wanted or needed any day of the year. How much should I spend? How intimate should the gift be? I didn't want any festive faux pas to wreck our relationship when everything was going so well. Perhaps Mum would have some good ideas.

10

THE DESCENT OF WENDY

With my tea tables stowed mostly in my back garden or inside the shop until spring, there was enough room on the front terrace of the shop for Mum to park her car alongside mine. Just as well, because hers was crammed full of knitted goods, plus lots of cellophane packages of unused yarn, eight balls to a bag. It looked as if she was hoping to offload some of the late Mrs Hardy's stock onto me. There's only so much knitting a woman can do, even a retired one like my mum. It would take me years to work my way through that lot. If this was just part of Mrs Hardy's leftover stock, she couldn't have run down her shop as much as Mum had told me.

Coloured packages and garments pressed against every window of her little red hatchback. If I hadn't known Mum was in the driving seat, I'd have struggled to spot her. She looked like the star prize in a lucky dip, or the only decent toy in one of those grab machines in amusement arcades. I wondered whether there'd be a lucky dip at the fair.

'Where's Wendy?' joked Danny as she turned off the engine.

As soon as Mum stepped out of the car, she rushed to give me a bear hug. I leaned into her, glad to breathe the familiar heady waft of her Yardley freesia eau de toilette. We'd never been very tactile since I'd grown up, but after the dangers I'd survived on her previous visit, we were making up for lost time. I was glad circumstances had conspired to bring us back together again. Perhaps if Steven hadn't left, and our floundering relationship was still drifting on, Mum and I would still be estranged, which would have been very sad.

When at last we let go of each other, Mum cried, 'Danny's turn!' She held out her arms, allowing him to sweep her up in a warm embrace, lifting her momentarily off her feet. Danny was a big hugger.

'Right, let's help you unload before it gets dark,' I suggested.

It was the first Saturday in December, the week before the fair, and at four o'clock in the afternoon, dusk was already falling, brightened only by the twinkling strings of fairy lights that had been springing up in front windows and gardens around the village.

Soon the little sitting room of the Curiosity Shop was a kaleidoscope of colour. We'd stacked completed garments on the sofa and armchairs, and the many packs of unused yarn like so many bright bricks against the wall. Most of these packs were not in festive colours, but tasteful soft natural shades that would match my shop stock. Just looking at the array of pretty pastels set my imagination going, and I pictured cosy throws and cushions made of granny squares artfully draped and scattered about my shop, once Christmas was over.

'This is what I've made for that dear little girl of Mr Praed's,' she declared, holding up a beautifully worked tunic in forest green. A scarlet belt had been knitted into the waist and a scatter of Fair Isle snowflakes hung in an arc from shoulder to shoulder. 'And here are the matching legwarmers and hat.'

The latter were made in the scarlet of the belt, with glistening snowflakes on the legwarmers and on the tip of the hat a sparkly white bobble so huge as to weigh it down at a jaunty angle. For some reason, they looked strangely familiar. I wondered whether she'd copied the design from a Disney or Pixar character.

'Tilly will love them, Mum,' I said with a smile. 'She'll be the best dressed elf in the whole fair. Thank you so much.'

Silent for a moment, Mum put her head on one side. 'You don't recognise them, dear, do you?'

I narrowed my eyes as I considered the cheery outfit.

'One of the Seven Dwarves?' I hazarded. 'Or a character from *Shrek*?'

'I first made up this pattern up long before Shrek was born,' Mum replied, distracting me for a moment with the thought of what Shrek's mum must have looked like.

'Sorry, Mum, I'm not very well up on children's films.' *Having been unable to have children myself*, was my unspoken subtext, but I didn't want to upset her or myself with this reminder.

'Think of real people,' said Mum. 'Think of the person you know best of all.'

Danny shot her a knowing look, then turned to me. 'She means you, you daft thing.'

Mum reached out to squeeze his hand. 'Exactly right, dear. This is the same pattern I made for you for your primary school pantomime all those years ago. It's even the same size.'

When I held the tunic up by the shoulders against me, I felt like a giant.

'We must tell that to Tilly,' I said. 'She'll find it highly amusing.'

Danny tugged the bobble on the hat, making it sparkle even more with reflected firelight. 'It'll make it extra special to her too.

Tilly's very fond of Alice, you know. Almost as fond of her as Robert is.'

Mum's eyes shone.

'Oh, don't encourage her,' I said. 'Robert and I are just good friends who like to spend time together.'

Mum and Danny exchanged disbelieving looks.

'And will Robert be at the fair next week?' asked Mum. She feigned innocence, but I suspected she was already planning her hat for our wedding.

I bit back a smile. 'Yes, he's playing Santa. Now let's find a good home for all this knitwear so we can actually sit on the sofa, and it's clear for me to sleep on tonight.'

'Actually, Alice, that won't be necessary,' said Danny. His tone was unusually shy. 'You see, when I told Jack that Wendy was coming, he invited me to stay with him so she can have my room. Just for now, you understand. This isn't a permanent fixture.'

If Jack had been there, I would have hugged him. To be honest, I hadn't been relishing another stretch of camping out on my sofa.

'Thanks, Danny, and say a big thank you to Jack from me too.'

'What are Jack's favourite colours, dear?' Mum asked Danny. 'I'll make him a nice warm scarf to say thank you.'

That gave me an idea: a hand-knitted jumper in a soft shade of blue would be the perfect Christmas gift for Robert. If I used some of Mrs Hardy's old stock, it would cost me only my labour and have no obvious commercial value. Whatever Robert bought me, he couldn't compare the prices and find my gift lacking. I could see just the right shade in the cellophane pack at the bottom of the pile by the door. I couldn't wait to get my needles out and get cracking.

11

SANTAS ON THE RUN

Much of the week that passed between Mum's arrival and the date of the fair she spent preparing for her stall. As well as sewing various buttons and other fasteners from my collection onto her otherwise completed garments, she knitted half a dozen more scarves. Then she handwrote beautiful price labels illustrated with sketches of holly and mistletoe and pinned one to every item. She raided my shop for suitable props to accessorise her display, such as the biggest wicker basket to hold rolled-up scarves and gloves and a clothes rail to display the sweaters on coat hangers borrowed from Danny's wardrobe.

'I'll iron all Danny's clothes before I hang them back up again,' she told me.

'You've got too much time on your hands, Mum,' I remarked, before realising how empty her days might have been without this project.

Vintage teapots on the dresser were soon modelling her range of tea cosies, and a couple of old china-faced dolls were recruited to model baby clothes.

I was beginning to realise Mum hadn't made all these especially for the fair. She must have been a one-woman knitting factory for some time before. Then I spotted a telltale price label bearing the name of Mrs Hardy's wool shop, The Woolgatherer, and I realised she'd been making garments for Mrs Hardy to sell in her shop. Quite likely, Mrs Hardy had been giving her the yarn for free, so Mum could have the fun of knitting the items, while Mrs Hardy would recoup her costs, plus a bit more, when she sold them. Only now did I remember that kind old Mrs Hardy had suggested this deal just after Dad died, as unofficial occupational therapy to help Mum deal with his loss. I may not have been able to fill the void left in Mum's life by Mrs Hardy's demise, but at least I could make her feel needed and valued through the calming process of knitting.

On the evening before the fair, Mum stood back from the kitchen table to admire for the umpteenth time her practice display. It looked even more stunning than the first few iterations she'd assembled earlier in the week, which Mum had photographed and sent to Jack Dauntless for the fair's marketing purposes.

Jack was the school tech whizz and provided online publicity for many village events. His Facebook posts for my sale of chess sets in the autumn had attracted loads of visitors from beyond the parish, some more welcome than others. For the last month he'd been posting a photo to promote a different Christmas fair stallholder each day. Seeing the photo of Mum's handiwork pop up on the fair's Facebook page had made me feel proud, like a mother seeing her child's school reports. It was as if I was parenting the parent already. Although Mum was seventy-five, I hadn't anticipated that happening just yet.

'Are you coming to watch the Santa Run before the fair opens, Mum?' I asked as she packed her wares and props into boxes and bags ready for the big day. 'It starts at ten o'clock and is expected to be all done by eleven when the fair opens its doors.'

Mum hugged a pile of paired gloves to her chest. 'I'm not sure I can, dear. Set-up time is between nine and eleven, and although I'm planning to be there from nine, and should be all set up by ten, I shan't want to abandon my stall once everything's been put out. So, I'll stay in the warm and give the run a miss, if you don't mind. You can take pictures and show me later at home.'

I lifted a box of china teapots gently onto the floor, keen to set the table for our tea now.

'It'll be fine leaving it unattended, Mum,' I advised her. 'It's not as if anyone's going to pinch anything. All your stuff will be perfectly safe with plenty of other people about the hall to keep an eye on things. This is Little Pride. Lots of people round here don't even lock their doors during the day.'

Mum surveyed her goods in silence. 'Besides, I might get a chill if I go out and stand about outside at this time of year. I don't want to be poorly just in time for Christmas.'

I gave up. If she wanted to spend all her time manning her stall, that was her decision.

'I'll go out and watch the start, if you don't mind, Mum,' I said. 'It ought to be quite a spectacle seeing a couple of hundred Santas tearing across the field. I wonder how easy it will be to tell them apart? I'd hate to go up and throw my arms around the wrong Santa, thinking it was Robert.'

* * *

As it turned out, plenty of runners were easily recognisable as not being Robert, because they were women. Their red-skirted costumes looked far less cosy than the men's classic red baggy trousers and tunics. On this dry but chilly morning, the fur edgings of the ladies' skirts and collars might have been all that stood between them and hypothermia, at least until they'd run far enough to get their circulation going. It took me a moment to spot Danny at the starting line, in red Lycra shorts beneath a baggy fur-edged tunic, thick red socks peeking out above his wellies, leaving his toned, dark knees exposed to the elements. Beside him stood Jack in an identical outfit. Their relaxed air suggested they were in it for fun, not prizes.

Search as I might for Robert, I couldn't spot him in the crowd, although my heart skipped a beat more than once when I thought I'd found him.

A familiar deep voice murmured behind me: 'Not the easiest identity parade, is it?'

As Robert took my hand, the white fur on the cuff of his red coat tickled my wrist agreeably.

'It reminds me of that scene in the film *Spartacus*. "I'm Santa Claus." "No, I'm Santa Claus!"' I squeezed his fingers, glad to warm my cold ones against his warm flesh. 'And all along, the real one's standing right next to me. Aren't I the lucky one?'

Before he could reply, the school's headmaster fired the sports day starting pistol, loaded with blanks, of course. Within seconds, hundreds of feet were thundering across the damp grass, heading for the gate that led from the recreation ground onto the high street.

'You can always spot the competitive runners if you know what to look for,' said Robert. 'They're the ones that slice the soles off their Wellington boots and slip the uppers over proper running shoes.'

I glanced down at his feet.

'That's one thing I don't have to worry about,' he said, 'as I'm not running in the race. I've decided the real Santa favours cosy Ugg boots. Don't let anyone tell you otherwise.'

'Ha! I suppose the real Santa's corporate sponsorship deals must be worth a fortune,' I joked.

As the Santas disappeared from view, Robert tugged at my hand. 'Come on, let's go inside and grab a coffee to warm up before they all return. I've got to be back here when the first runner comes in to hand out prizes, then it'll be a gruelling few hours' hard labour in my grotto. This might be my only chance for a caffeine fix until the fair is all over.'

Back inside the hall, we took a coffee to Mum at her stall, where the elfin Tilly was prancing about showing off her new outfit to the admiration of Mum and, on the adjacent stall, Maudie Frampton.

'You're a very good advertisement for my stall, dear,' Mum was telling her. 'I'm sure my jumpers will be flying off the table with you around.'

I spotted an opportunity that they'd both enjoy.

'I tell you what, Tilly, I bet my mum would love you to help her on the stall whenever you have a free moment.'

Mum nodded in approval.

Tilly surveyed all the other stalls for a moment, apparently assessing how much time she would need to do justice to the ones aimed at children of her age, such as the sweetie table, the Pin the Red Nose on Rudolph, and the bran tub – the rural equivalent of a lucky dip. A barrel was filled with actual bran, doubtless borrowed for the day from some village chickens.

'I'll try to fit it in, Alice's mummy,' she promised, before spotting a classmate waving to her beside the gingerbread stand and rushing off to join her.

'You'd better visit the ladies' before it starts, Mum,' I advised her. 'Once they let the public in, you're unlikely to get a break until it's all over bar the raffle draw. Village events like this tend to be very well supported, even without the import of a couple of hundred Santas from foreign parts.'

'Oh, are they from overseas, dear? Is this like a Father Christmas Olympics?'

I laughed, realising I had fallen into the locals' habit of tagging any from beyond the parish as foreign.

'Not really, just most of them aren't from Little Pride,' I explained. 'Anyway, the elite runners should be approaching the finishing line any minute now, so if you don't mind, I'll abandon you and watch all the Santas come in.'

At that moment, Robert approached me and caught my hand in his, to a smile of approval from Mum.

We reached the finishing post just as the first Santa appeared at the gate and entered the narrow strait that had been roped off with stakes and tapes borrowed from the village school sports cupboard. Everyone began to shout encouragement and clap and stamp their feet as the Santas began to stream across the muddy grass in a blur of red and white. Some charged along in an energetic finishing sprint, while others barely surpassed walking pace.

Sure enough, the fastest man and fastest woman both had expensive specialist running shoes concealed beneath the uppers of Wellington boots. Despite the cold drizzle that had started while they were running, some Santas had shed their tunics or wrapped them round their waists. Anyone not wearing a Santa hat was automatically disqualified, so the less fit runners, overheating, crossed the lines with cheeks almost as scarlet as their costumes.

It was all over very quickly. Robert awarded prizes to the first few finishers as one of the village schoolteachers wrote their names very neatly on handsome certificates. As the bulk of the runners finished the race in various clusters, I helped drop ribboned finishers' medals around their necks.

After catching their breath, some of the Santas headed straight to their cars to drive home. Others joined the back of the queue now snaking the length of the village hall, its windows thick with fake spray snow, waiting for the fair to officially open.

I had just dished out a medal to an elderly walker with a genuine long white beard when Jack Dauntless, still wearing his Santa gear, appeared from within the village hall and rang the old brass school handbell in the manner of a festive town crier.

'The Little Pride Christmas Fair is now ho-ho-hopen for business!' he projected in his best teacher's voice. 'Merry Christmas, everyone! Enjoy the rest of your day!'

Seeing the queue morph into an eager crowd surging in the double doors of the village hall, I cut round the back way to enter through the kitchen. I planned to sidle around the back of the stalls to help Mum. Just as well I did, as the hall was by then a colourful mass of seething bodies. Those not in Santa suits were otherwise festively dressed. The children favoured elf suits, reindeer onesies or nativity play costumes. PTA parents, grandparents and other carers sported tinsel halos or bright bobble hats above Christmas jumpers. After standing in the cold on the rec, the humid warmth from so many assembled bodies was overwhelming. As soon as I reached Mum's stall, I slumped down onto one of her two chairs. With the excitement of her sales taking off, Mum was as pink-cheeked as some of the post-run Santas.

'The fair's only been open five minutes, and already I've sold three jumpers, a tea cosy and a hot water bottle cover!' she said. She thrust a handful of change to Mrs Jorkins, who was hugging a tea cosy adorned with crocheted flowers to her chest. 'Someone was asking if they could buy the teapot too. Is it OK if I sell your things from the shop?'

'That would be wonderful,' I said with a grin. 'They should all have price labels on them already. Just keep a separate note of the takings.'

She tapped her clipboard to demonstrate that she was doing exactly that.

'If you need me to hold the fort for a bit, just say,' I told her.

'I'll be fine, dear, don't worry,' she reassured me. 'Besides, I've got my Tilly to help me.'

Tilly was quietly fiddling with the decorative buttons Mum had sewn onto some of the garments. I hoped her hands were clean.

I felt a bit superfluous. Perhaps Mum was still fondly remembering me at that age and in that outfit, even though I hadn't looked a bit like Tilly when I was a child.

'You go off now and have fun with your new friends, dear,' she insisted.

For a moment I feared she was going to give me some pocket money to spend, so I slipped away quickly and went to lend a hand washing up in the kitchen. With so many Santas now requiring cups of tea, there was a very different kind of race going on at the sink – to wash up used cups fast enough to free them up to fulfil new orders.

My wrinkled fingertips were looking like tiny brains by the time one of the PTA dads came to relieve me at the sink. I wandered over to the hatch to help myself to a much-needed and well-deserved cup of tea. As I savoured it in small sips, I surveyed the crowd, slightly reduced by now. Mum's stall was visibly sparser, and the bran tub, having yielded all its prizes, had been abandoned. Wondering which stall to visit first, I breathed in the wonderful cocktail of aromas now floating about the hall. Well, wonderful except for the sweatier Santas. An invigorating blend of sawdust, sap and polish emanated from the woodwork stall, vying for deliciousness with the spicy cloud arising from the urn of mulled wine. Shoppers were going around the room for a second or third time to make sure they hadn't missed anything. I hoped all the stallholders were doing as well as Mum.

Just then, cutting through the kaleidoscope of sounds, a piercing shriek rang from the direction of Mum's stall. Mum was nowhere to be seen, but at the adjacent table, Maudie Frampton was waving her stick in the air to raise an alarm.

'Stop that Santa! He's just stolen a scarf from Mrs Carroll's stall! Stop, thief. Stop him, someone, now!'

12

SANTA'S SOLO SPRINT

I set my unfinished cup of tea down on the serving hatch and jostled my way through the crowd to Mum's stall, which was now the focus of everyone's attention.

'Maudie, are you OK? What's happened?'

Maudie pointed her stick in the direction of the double doors. 'That man – a foreigner – made off with a lovely woolly scarf. A man dressed up like Father Christmas. If he could afford to buy that fancy-dress outfit, why couldn't he pay the fiver your mum wanted for her scarf? A bargain at the price, too.'

Exhausted by her tirade, Maudie fell back onto her chair, her arms and legs flopping as loose as a rag doll's. Several people, including Danny and Jack, were now clustering about her, asking if they could help.

'Can you describe him, Maudie?' I asked, already on the case. 'What did he look like?'

'Well, he was dressed like Santa, but wearing the scarf he stole off Mrs Carroll,' replied Maudie. 'He wrapped it round his neck, see, the minute he stepped away from the stall. Probably thought that would make people think it had been his all along.

Talk about brazen. Didn't even try to hide the fruits of his thieving.'

'What colour was the scarf?' added Jack.

That would narrow it down a bit.

'The scarf was as green as the grass in the spring, with a great big wooden button to fasten the ends together. Well, I call it a button, but it was shaped like some little creature – a sheep or a cat, I think.'

In the sea of Santas, not many of them would be wearing a grass-green, hand-knitted scarf fastened with a wooden animal button.

'Actually, it was a teddy bear,' said a child's voice at my elbow. Tilly was pulling at my sleeve. 'A brown teddy bear with eyes the colour of lime Rowntree's Fruit Gums.'

Danny and Jack exchanged glances.

'We'll go and look for him now, Alice,' said Danny, and they headed for the door.

'That's very observant, Tilly,' I congratulated her. 'You'd make a great detective. Are you sure?'

Tilly licked her forefinger and drew a cross over the centre of her elf tunic. 'Cross my heart and hope to die.'

I shuddered, not wanting to take the age-old playground vow literally. I'd seen too many dead bodies since I'd moved to Little Pride, and I didn't want to notch up any more.

'The reason I'm so sure is that I wanted Mummy to buy it for me,' Tilly continued. 'But she wouldn't because she said it was adult sized and would clash with my pink winter coat. I know I've already got a nice matching pink scarf, but really I just I wanted the little teddy bear. I'd have cut it off to play with. He was going to be a pet for my Barbie.'

Tilly's mum, Belinda, came to stand behind her and placed her hands gently on her daughter's shoulders.

'I'm sorry, darling, if I'd known some nasty man was going to steal it, I'd have bought it for you. How unkind to poor Alice's mummy, after all her hard work to knit it.'

At this point, Mum came bustling through the throng of shoppers, who by now had lost interest in the cause of Maudie's scream, perhaps disappointed the cause seemed so mundane. After all, there were plenty of other scarves on the stall, and Mum was only a fiver down on the lost transaction.

'Everything all right, dear?' Mum asked brightly as she returned to her station behind her stall.

I followed her and took her hand, easing us both down onto the chairs behind her table.

'No, Alice's mummy,' said Tilly. 'A wicked Santa just stole one of your scarves and ran off without paying for it.'

'Ran' was an exaggeration in this throng. It was probably more of a sidle, the multitude of fellow Santas camouflaging him from early detection.

'Did he, dear?' Mum reached across her stall to give Tilly's hand a comforting squeeze.

Maudie got up from her chair and shuffled over to stand beside Mum.

'I'm so sorry, Mrs Carroll, it's my fault.' Maudie's voice was shaky with remorse. 'You asked me to watch over your stall for you, but the devious blighter was too quick for me. He snatched it up and disappeared into the crowd before I could say "buttons".'

Maudie thrust her hand into her apron pocket and pulled out a crumpled fiver. 'Here, I owe you this for letting it get pinched. You must let me pay you for it.'

Mum whisked the banknote out of Maudie's hand and posted it back into the old lady's apron pocket.

'Nonsense,' Mum said briskly. 'You will do no such thing. If the poor soul needed a scarf and couldn't afford to pay for it, he is welcome to it, with my compliments. It's jolly cold out there at this time of year.'

Visibly moved, Maudie turned a watery gaze on me. 'Now I know where you get your kindness from, Alice Carroll.'

It was my turn to feel a little tearful.

'Shall I fetch you both a cup of tea to restore you after that nasty shock?' I offered.

'Good idea,' said Mum. 'Now, let's put that poor man behind us and get on with enjoying the afternoon. Maudie, it looks as if you're going to sell out of your preserves well before the end of the fair. They must have quite the reputation around here. What's your secret for a really good bramble jelly?'

Impressed by Mum's diplomacy, I left the two of them chatting pleasantly about jam-making and headed for the serving hatch. Once I'd brought them their teas, plus a plate of gingerbread men for a sugar boost, I turned my attention to catching up with Danny and Jack's search. I wished Robert wasn't otherwise engaged with his duties in Santa's grotto. Together we'd made a great pair of sleuths earlier in the year, and I could have done with his support right now.

I made a circuit of the hall, dodging between the stalls as I tried to find Danny and Jack in the sea of Santas. As one of the few Black Santas, Danny would have been easy to spot, but after my second fruitless lap, I gave up and decided to try outside.

As I headed out of the double doors, I was kicking myself for not realising the thief would most likely have fled the building rather than lingered indoors, despite the steady rain now falling.

Even if Danny and Jack had found him in the hall, they'd probably have taken him outside to reprimand him, so as not to spoil the fair's festive atmosphere.

I wondered whether the scarf was not the only thing he'd

pinched. With so many people clustering about the stalls, many of which were manned by a single seller, it would have been easy to sneak something from every stall undetected.

Weren't the media constantly reporting the rise in shoplifting these days? What better outfit to conceal stolen goods than a baggy Santa suit with deep pockets? And what better disguise, where half the browsers were similarly clad? At least at the Little Pride Christmas Fair, anyway. In the context of a supermarket, a solitary Father Christmas couldn't be more conspicuous.

I pushed my way past the raffle stall just inside the double doors, sited there to persuade all visitors to buy raffle tickets as they arrived. Recruiting the tenacious Suki to man it made it extra effective. Judging by the huge pile of tickets she was folding ready for the draw at the end of the fair, this strategy had been very successful. She looked up at me quizzically from behind the array of prizes, including a cheery child-sized Santa hat that Mum had donated as the obligatory raffle prize requested from every stallholder. But I had no time to talk to her now.

As I opened the double doors to the lobby, the chilly air hit me like a cold flannel to the face. Through the main door to the car park, I couldn't see a living soul, so I braced myself to check the car park, wishing I hadn't left my coat on one of the chairs behind Mum's stall.

Feeling thoroughly chilled within a minute of stepping outside, I glanced about the tightly packed car park, anticipating trouble later for those whose vehicles were blocked in by thoughtless double-parkers. Seeing no signs of life, I was about to go back inside when I caught the sound of muffled voices from behind the back of the hall. One of the voices was Danny's, rising above Jack's anguished murmur.

'Ambulance, please,' Danny was saying. 'That's our priority, but we'd better have the police as well. I'm afraid it looks as if the injured person has been assaulted with malicious intent.'

Now oblivious to the weather, I dashed through the open gates to the recreation ground and headed in the direction of Danny's voice, thinking, *Please let the victim not be Robert.* Surely he'd still be safe in his Grotto in the hall?

Skidding to a halt on the muddy grass, I let out a huge sigh of relief to see neither Robert, Danny nor Jack had been harmed. But my joy was short lived, when I realised Jack, crouched on his haunches with his back to me, was speaking in a low voice to another Santa who was sprawled at full length on the grass.

I ran round to kneel at his other side and took his hand. His fake white beard and drooping red hood covered too much of his face for me to see who it might be, but from the firm, unlined skin on the back of his hand, I guessed he was no older than me. I tried not to shrink back in horror at the new addition to his Santa suit: a scarf the colour of grass in spring, wrapped about his neck. It must have been tightly tied when the boys found him, because around what little I could see of his throat beneath the fake beard was a livid strip, already starting to turn from red to purple. I could hardly believe what I was seeing: a violent attack on a Santa Runner with a scarf made by my lovely mum's gentle hands. Whether or not this Santa was the same one who'd stolen the scarf didn't matter. All I cared about for now was this man's well-being.

Danny tucked his phone into the back pocket of his Lycra shorts, then slipped off his own Santa jacket and gently laid it over the prone man.

'As soon as we found him, we untied the knotted scarf,' said Danny in a low voice, while Jack continued to speak in a soft, comforting tone to the prostrate victim.

'Stay with me, Clive. Tell me how you're planning to spend

your Christmas this year. How did you fare in the Santa Run today? Was it your first time taking part? I don't think I've seen you run it before. It was my partner Danny's first time too.'

So his name was Clive. He must have been able to tell them that, but he seemed to be weakening by the moment. I didn't know of any Clives in Little Pride.

My concern for Clive didn't distract me from recognising that this was the first time I'd heard either Jack or Danny refer to each other as a partner. In these dire circumstances, I took a tiny grain of comfort from that.

Clive wasn't answering any of Jack's questions. With that wound to his throat, any attempt to speak must have sent a paroxysm of pain through his body. Who could blame him for saving his voice for something more important than small talk?

Then, 'Net,' he said, trying and failing to lift his head off the ground. 'Net,' he said again, but that was as far as he was able to go, before he lost consciousness.

13

EMERGENCY SERVICES

Jack grabbed Clive's wrist, wrapping finger and thumb around to find his pulse point.

'There's a pulse, but it's erratic.'

He placed a hand gently on Clive's chest, which was rising and falling feebly. Little puffs of condensation emanated from his open mouth, but his breathing was rapid and shallow.

'I don't think artificial respiration is appropriate yet,' whispered Danny. 'Just keep talking to him while I go to look for the ambulance. Hearing is the last sense to go.'

'I hope to goodness the ambulance can get through the car park,' I said. 'It's absolutely crammed. They might have to stretcher him out to the main road.'

As a siren approached up the high street, Danny darted off to flag it down and direct it to us.

'Hello, Clive, I'm Alice Carroll,' I said softly, to give Jack a break. 'Can you believe my mum named me Alice because she's a fan of Lewis Carroll's children's stories? She felt the coincidence of having married a Mr Carroll was too good an opportunity to miss. Who knows? Maybe that's why she married him!' I forced a little laugh. 'Clive's a good name, though – rugged and manly. I believe it only caught on because of the exploits of Clive of India, who helped found the East India Company. Which is odd really because Clive's first name was actually Robert. My mum was named after the character in J. M. Barrie's *Peter Pan*. Barrie made up the name Wendy by combining a diminutive of "little friend" or "fwend". What were my grandparents thinking?'

I didn't expect Clive to respond to my nervous prattle, but at least it might distract him from his pain.

Just as I was racking my brains for other facts about Clive of India, I heard the distinctive sliding sound of an ambulance van door over by the gate. I looked up to discover that thanks to the remarkable skill of its driver, the ambulance had squeezed through the car park and made it onto the muddy grass a few metres beyond us. Two paramedics were now following Danny towards us as he outlined what little we knew of the incident.

The boys and I stood back beside the van to let the paramedics set to work checking Clive's vital signs with various bits of medical kit, tapping their findings into an electronic tablet. After a few minutes one of them came over to speak to us. An official identification card on his breast pocket told us he was called Jeff.

'Is Clive a friend of yours?' asked Jeff. 'Is he from the village? Any family at hand?'

We all shook our heads.

'Sorry, no,' said Jack. 'There are lots of people here from beyond the parish today because of the Santa Run this morning. It's a 5K fun run with everyone dressed as Santa. There was a St John Ambulance here this morning for health and safety during the race, but it left after the last runner finished the race.'

'We haven't checked his pockets for identification or a mobile phone,' added Danny. 'We thought that was probably best left for the police when they get here. We only know he's called Clive because we managed to get it out of him when we first found him on the ground.'

'Did he say anything else that might help us?' asked Jeff.

'Nothing substantial,' said Jack, 'apart from something about a net. But I've no idea what kind of net he meant. Sports net maybe?' He nodded at the basketball hoop fixed to the end wall of the village hall. 'Or football net? There's a football pitch further down the field. Fishing net? Although there's no spot near here for fishing.'

'Maybe he meant the internet,' suggested Danny.

'OK, thanks, guys, we'll leave it there,' said Jeff, as a police car pulled up alongside the ambulance. 'We'll let the boys in blue work on his identity. I daresay the event organiser will give them his contact details from the entries database, which would probably also mention his next of kin. Meanwhile, our priority is to get our friend Clive to A & E to check for internal damage to his throat and neck. Better brace him up for the journey.'

Jeff stepped up into the van, emerging a moment later carrying a furled stretcher and a plastic neck collar.

For a moment, I wondered whether it would be unspeakably callous to ask if I could take the bear off the scarf for Tilly, before they took Clive away. If the police wanted to test the scarf for DNA, there'd surely be enough on there even without the teddy bear decoration.

But the question didn't arise, because as Jeff and his mate Charlie stretchered Clive into the ambulance, I spotted a loose thread hanging from near the bottom of the scarf – the thread Mum must have used to sew on the bear in question. The scarf was definitely Mum's handiwork. I recognised her distinctive use of linen stitch, which makes a finished article look as if it has been woven rather than knitted, hence the name. It also makes for very strong fabric, even stronger for her use of an acrylic yarn. I gulped. *All the better to strangle you with, my dear*, as the wolf in 'Red Riding Hood' might have said.

We lingered nearby as the two emergency services did their duty, ignoring the heavy rain now hammering down on us like bullets. Once the ambulance had departed, blue lights flashing, the police officers asked all three of us to step into the shelter of their car to make our statements.

The gist of their questioning to Danny and Jack, as first on the scene, was whether they'd seen a potential attacker running away.

'I think I noticed another Santa leaving the car park just before we turned the corner of the hall and found Clive,' said Danny.

'But then we've been seeing Santas running about all day,' added Jack. 'So that doesn't narrow the field of suspects much.'

'Something Danny and Jack didn't mention was the toggle missing from the scarf,' I said when it was my turn. The younger officer had already bundled the bloodstained scarf into a clear plastic evidence bag. 'It was shaped like a bear, sewn on for decoration. I wonder whether that might be of importance.'

In their silence, I continued. 'It had green eyes set into the wood, and was more the size of a toggle than a button, like you might find on a duffel coat.'

The officers exchanged bemused glances.

'I very much doubt it's significant, Ms Carroll,' said the senior officer. 'But if a brown bear turns up, we'll be sure to let you know.'

I gritted my teeth at his wry manner. Would he have

dismissed my suggestion so readily if Danny or Jack had made it? But then perhaps the police need the odd bit of humour to get them through the stress of their duties. They were probably having to deal with grim incidents like this every day. Who was I to criticise?

'We'll be in touch again in a day or two to ask you to sign your statements, once we've typed up these notes,' he continued. He turned to face Jack. 'You say you can give us the names of the stallholders, sir, in case we wish to question them?'

'Yes, Officer, I should be able to download them from the school computer on Monday. But if you need them sooner, you'll find them all on the event's Facebook page.'

'If it's of any help, I could put a notice in the *Little Pride Parish News* to bring in any further witnesses of the theft or the assault,' I offered, hoping to assert some personal authority after their patronising comment about the missing button. 'I'm its editor, and the copy deadline for the January edition is next Saturday.'

The two police officers exchanged condescending glances. 'Thanks, madam, but I think our usual channels on the internet will yield swifter results than the village jungle drums.'

I pursed my lips. That was their loss.

As Danny, Jack and I climbed out of the police car, the officers bade their goodbyes.

'Not if you want evidence from anyone who never goes near the internet,' I retorted as the police car pulled away. 'Like Mr and Mrs Jorkins or Maudie Frampton and her husband, or Nell Littlewood. Dismiss older witnesses at your peril, my friends.'

As we stood watching the police car manoeuvre through the packed car park, I folded my arms in defiance. The wave of cold it sent across my chest made me realise my jumper was wet through.

Danny put his arm around me on one side and Jack on the other, and we trudged, dripping, back into the village hall.

'I'll break the sad news to the headmaster,' said Jack. 'Then he can determine how to announce it to the community without cutting short the fair or frightening the children.'

For once, I was thankful to relinquish a task to a man.

14

WARMING UP

When Mum saw the state of me as I approached her stall, she didn't pause to ask questions. She just instructed Danny, Jack and me to go straight home and put on warm, dry clothes. The fair was nearly over in any case, and Suki was just shouting out that she'd be drawing the raffle in five minutes' time. After leaving our raffle tickets with Mum, we charged down the high street through the pouring rain to the Curiosity Shop. We couldn't possibly have got any wetter.

Although Danny was staying at Jack's for the duration of Mum's visit, he'd left most of his stuff in his room in my house. So, all three of us headed upstairs to get out of our wet things and into dry.

'Just bring all your wet clothes down and bung them in the washing machine,' I called to the boys through Danny's door. 'I'll stick a load on straight away.'

Not planning to go out again that evening, I changed into some fleecy tartan pyjamas, dressing gown and slippers, before heading downstairs to light the wood burner in the front room. Then I dumped my own damp clothes in the washing machine.

There was no point in drying them. We'd all got very muddy tending to poor Clive where he lay on the ground. I just hoped Danny and Jack's Santa suits were colourfast.

By the time the boys came downstairs, Jack looking as if he was wearing his big brother's hand-me-downs due to his narrow frame, I was snuggled down beneath a blanket, interrogating the internet for anything to do with grass-green scarves. I was rather clutching at straws here for want of any better ideas, but I was exploring whether Clive had been trying to tell us that the reason he'd stolen the scarf would be revealed on the 'net', as he kept saying. I wasn't sure how this could be, and tried to dream up possible scenarios.

Could there be some kind of charity appeal to steal scarves and give them to the homeless? That didn't sound exactly charitable towards the victims of the theft. Was there a vendetta against green scarves as if they were some kind of fashion crime? There's no knowing what might go viral on the internet. Just think of the ice bucket challenge a few years ago. If indeed Clive had been the scarf thief. There were plenty of other Santas about who might have stolen it. A different Santa might have taken it from Mum's stall, wrapped it round his own neck to try to pass it off as his own, and only later taken it off to use as a weapon against Clive.

I confess, the police officers' lack of interest in the scarf made me all the more determined to discover why a stolen scarf should be used as a murder weapon.

If indeed it was an assault with murderous intent. But I couldn't imagine that awful wound to be self-inflicted, no matter how many followers on TikTok were egging you on to tighten your scarf as much as you dared before blacking out. Besides, Clive was a grown-up. An adult's natural instinct for self-preservation should have kicked in long before he could have choked himself.

'What, no drinks?' asked Danny in mock horror as Jack settled down into one of the armchairs, holding his cold-reddened hands to the blazing fire to warm them.

'Feel free to fetch some, Danny,' I replied. 'You know where everything is.'

By now I was checking the main social media platforms in turn to see whether #scarf or #scarves or even #greenscarf was trending. It was a little rude of me not to make small talk with Jack, but I was on a mission now and determined to find a useful lead.

I didn't notice Jack pick up my *Chess for Simpletons* book from the shelf beneath the coffee table and open it at the bookmark until a one-word exclamation made me drop my phone and stare at him.

'Netsook,' he read from the Highbere Museum leaflet I'd been using as a bookmark. 'What's netsook when it's at home?'

I closed my eyes and shaded them with my hand for a moment as his inadvertent revelation sank in.

'It's pronounced "net-soo-key",' I said at last. 'Or at least, that's what we used to call it when I worked at Broadwick Museum. That's the Japanese word for the carved toggles they used in the olden days to attach purses to the belts of their kimonos.'

'You mean they didn't have pockets?' he replied, passing me the leaflet when I reached my hand out to him. 'I don't know, they've invented all those clever things such as electric cars and camera phones, yet they didn't think of sewing pockets into their kimonos? I hate having clothes with no pockets.'

'I'm with you on that one,' I said, thrusting my hands deep into the pockets of my dressing gown.

Danny came in from the kitchen with a tray bearing three

mugs of hot chocolate and two glasses of brandy. He's even teetotal in a time of a crisis.

'Hey, what's all the shouting about?' he asked, setting the tray on the coffee table and dropping onto the sofa beside me.

I had been so excited at Jack's inadvertent revelation that I hadn't noticed how loudly I had spoken.

'Jack has just given me the most amazing inspiration,' I said slowly.

'Yes, he can have that effect on a person,' replied Danny, winking at Jack.

'Danny, I'm serious,' I scolded him. 'What if that was no ordinary button on that scarf? For all we know, it might have been valuable. Perhaps one of those old Japanese carvings that men used to fasten things onto the belts of their kimonos before they adopted Western dress.'

Danny and I had once helped mount a modest exhibition of Japanese woodblock prints at Broadwick, and we'd both learned a lot about Japanese culture from that event.

Danny's jaw dropped. 'You mean netsuke? If so, when Clive kept saying "net", maybe he was trying to say "netsuke" but his injury stopped him from being able to get the whole word out.'

As he watched us, Jack turned his head back and forth like a spectator at a tennis match. 'But where would your mum have got a netsuke?'

I shrugged. 'All her knitting yarn came from Mrs Hardy's wool shop. But although Mrs Hardy sold buttons along with other items of haberdashery, she never stocked anything as valuable as netsuke, not even modern reproductions.'

I remembered lingering over Mrs Hardy's display of long, clear, plastic tubes of buttons when I still lived at home, choosing fastenings for the garments I'd knitted, but I'd never seen anything that fancy. Besides, you'd never get a netsuke through a normal buttonhole. Presumably that was why my mum had sewn this one on simply as a decoration instead.

'Did Mrs Hardy have any connections with Japan? Perhaps her father was stationed there after the war or something?' asked Danny. 'Or maybe she'd inherited a collection of netsuke from a wealthy relative dating back to the days when Japan first opened up to the West. Back then, in mid-Victorian times, Europe went mad for Japanese stuff. You know, for kimonos and fans and lacquered furniture and willow-patterned porcelain. It was so influential over Western tastes and artists that they coined a name for it: Japonisme.'

'And Gilbert and Sullivan wrote *The Mikado*,' added Jack.

I hadn't put him down as a musical theatre fan, but now he said it, I could picture him on stage in full costume in the cast of a Gilbert and Sullivan operetta. I was looking forward to getting to know him better.

'I'll have to ask Mum when she gets back,' I said. 'Maybe one of my village friends, such as Maudie Frampton or Mrs Jorkins, had one or more pieces of netsuke tucked away in the button boxes I bought from them. I can't believe I didn't notice them when I was sorting them out, because they would have been so much bigger than the average button. But there were an awful lot of buttons, and I was constantly being interrupted.'

Danny opened up the gate-folded leaflet and studied it more carefully. 'What's this Highbere Museum leaflet doing here anyway?' His brow furrowed.

'The postman brought it the other day,' I said. 'It's a circular.'

'Highbere Museum must be very well off if it can afford that kind of leaflet drop so far beyond its immediate catchment area. I know it's reputed to have received a lot of lottery money, but even so.'

'Coo-ee!' came a cry from the shop. It was Mum arriving back from the fair. With a broad smile, she breezed into the sitting room carrying a couple of hessian shopping bags containing her few remaining wares. 'Robert kindly collected the props I borrowed from your shop, and he will pop round with them later.'

She perched on the rocking chair by the fire, looking pleased with herself.

'I made over £500 today,' she continued. 'Mmm, that cocoa looks good.'

'I'll make you one now, Wendy,' said Danny. 'Jack, you come and help me.'

At once I realised he was providing a discreet opportunity for me to tell Mum about the awful business with Clive. Wary as I was of upsetting her, I was grateful for his thoughtfulness. Small mercies.

15

THE GREEN SCARF

'You won a prize in the raffle, dear,' Mum said before I could speak.

'What fun,' I said, not feeling it. 'What did I win?'

Mum's eyes twinkled with mischief. 'One of Coralie's beautiful button necklaces. I know that's rather coals to Newcastle, given how many buttons you still have to find good homes for. I hope you don't mind, but in your absence, I gave it to Tilly to make up for missing out on that little teddy bear scarf she was hankering after. She was thrilled.'

'You spoil that child,' I teased her.

'So, a successful day all round,' said Mum. 'My stall very nearly sold out.'

I grimaced. 'It depends how you look at it.' I hesitated, wanting to let her down gently. 'You know we went off in search of the man who stole the green scarf.'

Mum nodded encouragingly. 'Yes, thank you, dear. Did you have any luck finding him? Did you manage to get the scarf back or to extract the fiver from him? Of course, if he really couldn't afford a warm scarf but just needed one, I don't begrudge it to him, but it would have been nice if he'd asked first.'

I remembered that Mum and Mrs Hardy and some other Woolgatherer customers made a habit each winter of knitting scarves, hats and gloves and leaving them in bus shelters and waiting rooms for needy people to help themselves.

I gulped down the rest of my brandy.

'We found him all right, but I'm afraid neither he nor the scarf were in great shape. Someone had used your scarf to assault him.' I didn't like to be more graphic than that. To know it had been used as a garrotte would have horrified her. 'Then they left him lying in the mud behind the hall, apparently taking with them the toggle you'd sewn onto the scarf.'

'How odd,' said Mum. 'Is the poor chap OK?'

'That's for the hospital to say,' I replied. 'We called an ambulance as he was in such a bad way, and they put a surgical collar on him and rushed him off to A & E.'

Mum put her hand to her throat. Although I had chosen my words carefully, she didn't need to be a genius to work out how a scarf might be weaponised.

'Goodness,' was all she could say, and I was glad when Danny returned with a mug of cocoa and another glass of brandy to fortify her.

After a few strengthening sips of cocoa, Mum went into analytical mode. 'But why? Who was he? It makes no sense. Especially at a Christmas fair, where everyone is just bent on having fun.'

Danny perched on the arm of the sofa beside me.

'We think it could be for financial gain,' he began, 'because we suspect that the toggle you'd sewn onto the scarf for decoration was no ordinary button.'

'I confess I thought that myself,' said Mum. 'It was rather

fancy. Almost like a child's toy. Very three-dimensional, and just the right size to fit comfortably into a child's hand. No wonder Tilly fell for it. You used to like tiny toys like that when you were a little girl, Alice. You used to go to school with a little dolly tucked inside your blazer pocket.'

'Oh, yes, Ruby Rainbow!'

I could still picture the little plastic doll in her stripy dress who secretly accompanied me to primary school every day until I was about eight years old. I used to slip my hand into my pocket to hug her whenever I was anxious. I wondered what had become of her.

'So where did you get the fancy button from, Wendy?' Danny was managing to stay more focused than I was. 'Was it part of the wool shop stock you inherited, or did you find it in one of Alice's button boxes?'

'Oh, it can't have come from Mrs Hardy's shop, as I didn't bring any buttons with me. Alice said she had plenty here for me to use. But as to which box it came from...' Mum sat back, clutching her forehead as if a migraine was incoming. 'I've chosen so many buttons from so many of her boxes and tins these last few days, I'm not sure I can recall.'

Try, Mum, please try, I urged her silently, not wanting to make her feel anxious by saying it aloud. My thoughts were interrupted by the buzzing of my phone. I grabbed it from the coffee table and darted out through the kitchen to the back garden, the best place to get a signal on my property. I only remembered when I was standing on the puddly patio that I was still wearing my bedroom slippers.

A few minutes later, I squelched back into the sitting room, feeling more chilled than was natural for that short exposure to the now lighter rain.

'That was the police,' I told the assembled group.

Jack was now sitting cross-legged on the hearth rug, lapping up the warmth of the roaring flames and leaning against Danny's legs.

'It's about Clive. They said the paramedics did all they could in the ambulance, but I'm afraid they couldn't save him. The police are now treating his assault as attempted murder.'

16

THE DEATH OF SANTA

The silence that had fallen on my sitting room while we processed the sad news was shattered by a sharp rap at the shop door. No one else moved, and everyone looked at me.

'I'll go,' I said. After all, it was my shop. I dreaded seeing who might be there – the police? The local press? Villagers who had heard the news of the attack on Clive and wanted to hear our version of events and get an update on developments?

With any luck, it would just be more carol singers. We'd had three lots round in the last week, and it was always heartwarming to hear them.

It was none of those. I threw myself against Robert's chest and wrapped my arms around him. Robert put down the two big bags of Mum's props he was carrying and held me tight, stroking my hair and kissing the top of my head as I sobbed quietly. Suddenly everything was catching up with me.

'From the window of my grotto, I saw the ambulance and the police car arrive and leave,' he said gently. Santa's grotto for the fair's purposes was the little room behind the stage at the end of the village hall that faced the high street. 'The chair of the PTA told me what had happened after the general public had gone, and the stallholders were packing up. I helped to stow some tables and chairs away, then went home to have a shower. I was pretty sticky after dealing with all those sweet-fuelled children all afternoon. I also needed to change out of my Santa suit before coming round here. I thought you'd probably seen enough Father Christmases for one day.'

'Enough Father Christmases to last a lifetime.' I pulled back from his chest. 'If you'd come round here still in your Santa suit, I would have thought I was seeing a ghost.'

Robert took a step back. 'A ghost? You don't mean…'

I nodded as I tried to stifle a sob, which emerged instead as a hiccup.

'I'm afraid so. I've just taken a phone call from the police to tell me poor Clive, the Santa who was attacked, died before he reached the hospital. His surname was Thatcher by the way. They told me that too.'

Robert closed his eyes for a moment, as if offering up a swift prayer. 'Poor man. But Clive Thatcher, you say? I don't know anyone called Clive Thatcher. There are no Clives of any kind in Little Pride or even Great Pride, as far as I know. He must have been one of the visiting runners.'

'I thought so too. When Danny and Jack found the poor man, he could barely speak. Someone had tried to garrotte him with one of Mum's scarves, and they very nearly finished the job on the spot. All Clive kept saying was something to do with a net, and we've only just worked out that he actually meant a netsuke – in fact, the netsuke that Mum had sewn onto the green scarf thinking it was just a fancy big button. But we'd better go through to the sitting room. Danny and Jack are there with Mum, and they'll all be wondering who was at the door. We were half expecting it to be the police, asking for further statements, or someone like Suki Price, seeking ammunition for the village gossip machine.'

Robert closed the door behind him and put a comforting arm around my shoulders. We crossed the dark shop together and entered the sitting room that lay bathed in light beyond.

I'd expected Mum, Danny and Jack still to be sitting in stunned silence as they had been when I got up to answer the door. Instead, they were all talking at once in animated fashion.

Danny was elaborating on the Victorians' passion for all things Japanese and citing Edmund de Waal's memoir *The Hare with Amber Eyes*, a compelling history of the flood of netsuke into European cultural centres, and their subsequent dispersal.

Jack was pressing Danny to elaborate on what was so special about Highbere Museum compared to Broadwick City Museum.

Mum was reciting a list of all the most interesting and unusual buttons she'd sewn onto her festive wares since arriving at my house, and counting them off on her fingers.

On seeing Robert, they all stopped mid-sentence.

'Hello, all,' said Robert, with a wave of greeting to them. 'Alice has just told me the sad news about the death of Santa Clive.'

When Danny got up to make room for Robert on the sofa, Jack stood up too, and Danny signalled to him to go to the kitchen to rustle up drinks for our new arrival.

I sat down beside Robert, glad of the warmth of his body, fresh from the shower, as I leaned against him. Despite the cocoa and brandy, I still felt quite chilled from my earlier soaking.

'Just before you arrived, Robert, we were speculating whether the theft of Mum's scarf was somehow connected with the fact that it was accessorised with what may turn out to be a valuable piece of antique Japanese netsuke.'

'I'm familiar with netsuke,' said Robert. 'My great-grandfather had a small collection.'

I passed the museum flyer to Robert, who examined the pictures of its Japonisme exhibition.

'I suppose it's not out of the question that somehow a netsuke or two might have ended up in one of those button boxes you've been buying up lately, Alice,' he continued. 'If I've had a few handed down to me, so might anyone else around here. They're not all museum pieces, though. There's a huge variation of quality and materials. You can buy modern reproductions for about thirty quid a pop.'

'That's a lot to pay for a button,' murmured Mum.

'I remember playing with my grandmother's button box when I was a child,' said Robert. 'I used to find all sorts of things in it that shouldn't have been there, from my grandfather's service medals to empty bullet cases. A button box would be an obvious place for stray netsuke to end up, if they got into the hands of someone who didn't appreciate their heritage. After all, they do have holes drilled in them, just like buttons, to thread a cord through. It's an easy enough mistake to make.'

Mum's face lit up. 'Ooh, do you still have your grandmother's button box, Robert? I'd love a rummage through. Perhaps I could find another animal-shaped button that Tilly might like just as much.'

Robert smiled at her enthusiasm. 'It's probably up in my loft somewhere, or in my daughter Belinda's, over in Great Pride. When I have a moment, I'll search it out and pass it on to you.'

'But if Clive recognised the bear as a valuable netsuke,' said Danny, 'why didn't he just pay Wendy, like any other customer, and acquire the scarf fair and square?'

'Quite,' said Jack. 'It would have been a great bargain, like the kind of story you see on television programmes like *Antiques Roadshow*, when someone pays a few quid for a grubby old painting at a car boot sale, and it turns out to be a genuine van

Gogh. Think of all the trouble it would have saved him. Not to mention his life.'

'I'm just wishing I'd given the green scarf to Tilly at the start of the fair, when she showed an interest,' said Mum mournfully. 'Then perhaps Clive would still be alive and kicking.'

I wished she had too now. I made a private vow never to begrudge her burgeoning friendship with Tilly again. No one, no matter how cute and winsome, can replace a real daughter in a mother's affection, and Mum had plenty of love for us all.

'Don't blame yourself for a moment, Wendy,' counselled Robert. 'There's no way you could have known what was going to happen.'

The tense lines on Mum's face relaxed slightly.

'You're right, Robert,' she said. 'Besides, he didn't even approach the stall while I was there. I went to the ladies' and asked Maudie Frampton to keep an eye on my stall while I was gone, as her table was right next to mine. I only meant for her to take payment if someone wanted to buy something in my absence, rather than have to wait for me to come back. The threat of shoplifters never crossed my mind. The first Maudie noticed of the fellow was the sudden movement of snatching the scarf from the front corner of my table, before he plunged back into the crowd and vanished. I told her not to feel bad about it. It's not as if she could have tackled him physically at her age, especially from behind her stall.'

'And to be fair,' I added, 'Maudie did sound the alarm straight away. Danny and Jack could hardly have found Clive any quicker or acted faster at calling the emergency services.'

'Thanks, Alice,' said Jack, grasping Danny's hand.

They must have been suffering pangs of misplaced guilt at not being able to do more to save Clive.

'Whoever he was, Clive didn't deserve to die such a painful death for the theft of something priced a fiver,' said Robert.

'It's not as if the yarn cost me anything,' said Mum. 'And besides, it was super-chunky, knitted on big needles, so it only took me a couple of hours to make.'

'Your time is worth far more than £2.50 an hour, Mrs Carroll,' put in Jack kindly.

'Yes, but if Wendy charged even minimum wage for the amount of time it takes to produce a garment, it would price her out of the market,' said Robert, who never seems to take his business head off. 'Think how cheaply you can buy factory-made scarves. Not that they're anywhere near as nice.'

'Anyway, Mum,' I continued, 'the point is, the yarn may not have been worth much, but supposing the ornament was a collectible antique worth thousands. Then the stakes would have been much higher, and the theft worth a greater risk than pinching a plain, unadorned scarf.'

Mum folded her arms across her chest. 'Well, all the more reason this Clive fellow should have just put his hand in his pocket and paid me my rightful fiver. Then both of us would have been happy.'

We couldn't disagree with her reasoning.

'Alice, have you put your theory to the police?' asked Robert.

I shook my head. 'I tried, but they more or less laughed me down.'

Robert grabbed my hand with both of his. 'All the more reason for us to investigate this matter ourselves. If the police can find another valid motive, and catch Clive's killer as a result, all well and good. But if you're right, and they're not even going to follow up your hunch, they're never going to bring the murderer to justice. I say we take it up together, Alice, and see what we can do. We've nothing to lose. Besides, we're good at sleuthing. We make a great team.'

A murmur of unanimous consent circled the room, and I fetched the brandy bottle from the kitchen to replenish our glasses.

'I'll drink to that,' I declared, and sank back onto the sofa, nestled against Robert's warm body, to consider where to start.

17

BUTTON HUNTERS

Next morning, Mum kindly offered to man the shop – open on Sundays in December from ten till four to make the most of the Christmas market – while Robert and I put together a plan to find Clive's killer. Robert had invited me to brunch at his house to ensure I didn't get sidetracked by the shop, on the proviso that Mum would call my mobile if she had any problems with customers or stock.

As Robert drizzled maple syrup over our fluffy fresh pancakes and sweet-cured Canadian bacon, I headed a page in my notebook and numbered the lines.

'OK, so let's make a list of questions we need to answer as the starting point of our investigation,' I said.

'Fire away, Sherlock,' said Robert, pressing down the plunger in an aromatic cafetière of fresh coffee standing between our place settings at his kitchen breakfast bar.

I wriggled a little on my seat, full of my own self-importance at being assigned the lead role in our sleuthing partnership, even if only in jest. Here is what I wrote:

1. *Who was Clive anyway, and where did he come from?*
2. *What exactly was the decoration on the scarf – valuable netsuke or worthless tat?*
3. *If a valuable antique, where did Mum get it from?*
4. *Was the decoration the reason Clive wanted the scarf, or did he simply grab the nearest one as it was easiest to steal?*
5. *Was Clive a genuine Santa Run racer, or was the Santa suit a disguise for a more sinister purpose?*
6. *If not desirous of the scarf simply to keep out the cold, why did Clive steal it?*
7. *If stealing it to gain access to the antique netsuke, or whatever it was, was this an impulsive theft or pre-planned?*
8. *If pre-planned, how did he know it was going to be on Mum's stall and where to find it?*
9. *Why didn't he just pay the marked price for it?*
10. *Assuming he was after the netsuke, was he stealing it to sell on himself, or to order for an operator further up the criminal food chain?*

'That's a pretty comprehensive list, Alice,' said Robert, passing me the cream jug for my coffee. 'I have only one question to add: where on earth do we start?'

I picked up my knife and fork, unable to resist any longer the delicious scents arising from my breakfast plate. Only now did I realise how hungry I was and why. In the heat of the previous evening's analysis of the day's events, we'd somehow forgotten to eat a proper tea, making do with late-night toast instead, slathered with some of Maudie Frampton's legendary bramble jelly.

'That's a very good question,' I said, arranging narrow rashers of bacon evenly across the top of my stack of pancakes. 'I suggest Clive's identity. I asked the hospital, but they wouldn't tell me any more until his next of kin had identified him. I guess the police will release that information when they're ready. In the meantime, perhaps the second most important question is where did the button come from? Was it from Nell's old stock, or was it in one of the various button boxes I've acquired from villagers? If we only had a photograph of it, that would make life easier.'

'We'll just have to work with what we've got,' replied Robert. 'Still, it should be the most straightforward question to answer, so we might as well motivate ourselves by starting off with the low-hanging fruit. Who exactly have you bought button boxes from?'

I helped myself to a couple of strawberries from the pottery dish beside the cafetière and bit into one. I don't know where Robert sourced strawberries in December – definitely not from Suki's stores, which sold only seasonal goods – but these smelled and tasted far more delicious than they ought to have done in the middle of an English winter. I wiped a trickle of its pink juice from the corner of my mouth before replying.

'Maudie was the first, then Mrs Jorkins, then the vicar's wife,' I replied. 'In that order.'

'Then we'd better make a little trio of visits, if you can bear it,' said Robert. 'Although I realise we risk exposing ourselves to a grilling about yesterday's sad event, it'll be easier and more tactful to do this in person rather than on the phone.'

'Do you think they'll be offended if we call round on a Sunday? Especially at the vicarage?'

I knew some locals still held that the Sabbath was a day of rest – or at least of staying home and doing what they liked. A few people had expressed surprise or even dismay that I sometimes opened my shop on Sundays, but as its previous owner

Nell had counselled me, it was my shop, and I should keep whatever hours I liked, just as she had.

Robert shook his head. 'Provided we avoid core Sunday dinner time and afternoon nap time, we should be fine. And if we knock at the door and there's no answer, we can always try again tomorrow. I've no work commitments until after New Year's Day now, so treat me as your reinforcements, and I'll be happy to help.'

That made me feel better.

'We mustn't forget to consult Coralie,' I put in. 'I wonder whether she found any netsuke-type toggles in the buttons I gave her. Goodness, it hadn't occurred to me before, but what if the raid on Coralie's house wasn't by a kid cross about his haircut, or a random button collector, but by someone who thought she had valuable netsuke among her craft materials?'

I paused for a moment while I let that sink in.

'It could be that this wasn't the only piece of netsuke we had,' I continued. 'What if we had more of them? A whole collection. While sadly Clive can't return to steal any more, we can't assume that he was just an eccentric collector, willing to go to criminal lengths to add new pieces to his collection. If he's part of a gang, rather than a sole operator, other members might come to pick up where he left off. So, if we find any similar pieces, we ought to keep them out of harm's way until we've answered some of our other questions. If we've inadvertently split a valuable collection, we ought to reassemble them quick.'

'Do you have a safe in your shop?' asked Robert, topping up our coffee cups.

'Closest thing I've got to a safe in my shop is my till.'

Robert chuckled. My till was a vintage brass one, converted from its original currency of pounds, shillings and pence to accommodate decimalisation.

'Just as well I have one in my house, then,' he said. 'Which of course you are welcome to use any time. By the way, do you know exactly what the bear looked like? Do you think you could do some kind of identikit sketch? It might help jog the ladies' memories if you can at least give them a rough idea of what it looked like.'

'Tilly wanted to make it a pet for her Barbie doll's house, which gives us an idea of its size.' I held up my thumb and fore-finger a couple of inches apart. 'I think its shape was truer to nature than Barbie. It was more like one of those little toy zoo animals you can buy, only made of dark wood rather than plastic. I'll ask Mum. She will probably have a better memory of it from sewing it onto the scarf.'

I laid my knife and fork together across my empty plate. 'I'd rather not have to ask Tilly, although knowing Mum's artistic skills, or lack of, Tilly might produce a better sketch.'

'Art isn't only about drawing,' Robert reproved me. 'Wendy's a very skilful knitter.'

I had to agree. In fact, I had been rather proud of the fine display of Mum's knitwear on her stall the previous day. Hers was one of the most impressive stalls in the hall. I made a mental note to tell her at an opportune moment.

But first, we had a murder mystery to solve.

18

MUM'S EVIDENCE

I pulled my mobile out of my dress pocket and touched speed-dial for Mum. She answered after a few rings. She still hasn't really mastered mobile phone technology, and I had to remind her to go outside to get a decent signal. It might have worked better just to shout over Robert's wall to her.

'It's only me, Mum,' I began. 'Robert and I have just been wondering whether you could give us a good description of the netsuke bear you sewed on that scarf.'

I could almost hear Mum beaming down the phone. 'I can do one better than that, dear. I can give you a photograph.'

'What?' I almost dropped my phone. 'How?'

'I took a picture of it for Jack on my mobile,' she said, just a touch smug. 'Jack asked me for one for the advertising he was doing for the fair. Don't you remember? He asked every stall-holder to provide a photo of something that would be on their stall the week before the show, so that he could put them all on the event page he'd set up on Bookface.'

I bit my lip to stop myself from laughing.

'Awfully nice of him. It must have taken him ages, on top of all his marking and lesson preparation. He's a very thoughtful boy, dear, to make sure people were aware of every single stall before they even set foot in the fair. Especially useful for those whose stalls were in less advantageous positions. Mind you, I was very happy with where mine was, right next to Maudie's. Just about everyone came to buy a jar of something from Maudie, and they couldn't help but notice my stall next door.'

How kind the villagers were. Maudie was very hard up, and I guessed she depended upon the proceeds of her stall to fund her Christmas dinner and gifts.

I remembered now that Jack had asked me to take the photo, and I'd forgotten.

'So you took a photo on your phone, Mum?'

Mum had a history of failed phone photography. Her gallery was full of pictures of her feet or the insides of her pockets and handbags.

'Yes, dear, and Jack said it's a very good one. Danny's been giving me lessons. Honestly, those two are like the sons I never had.'

I closed my eyes. Perhaps the daughter she did have should have taught her phone photography instead of laughing at what she produced under her own steam.

'I'll pop back in a minute to send it from your phone to mine,' I said. 'So that I can show it to the button-box ladies Robert and I are planning to visit this afternoon.'

'No need, dear,' she said brightly. 'Danny's also taught me how to send photos to people. That's how I got it to Jack when he needed it.'

Of course. What a terrible daughter I was.

'Just a moment, dear.'

When that moment had elapsed, my phone pinged, and a notification popped up to alert me to the delivery of a new photo.

I opened it straight away. In pride of place at the front of a practice display of Mum's knitwear laid out on my kitchen table was the green scarf, adorned with a carved wooden bear with glinting lime-green eyes. Not only was the bear's shape and pose naturalistic, but its coat was brought to life by the tiniest of carved lines to denote fur. The eyes glinted in response to the flash of the phone's camera.

Now that I looked carefully, it was obvious that this was a very special piece of craftwork. Why had I been so stupid as to not notice it in among the buttons?

'Thanks, Mum, you've done a great job,' I told her.

'Have I, dear?' She sounded surprised. I really ought to praise her more often. 'Well, as long as you're happy. Will you be stopping by here for lunch?'

I glanced at the time on my phone screen as I patted my pancake-filled tummy. 'Probably not, so shut the shop whenever you like to grab some lunch from whatever you can find in the fridge, and I'll be home in time to cook us a nice dinner.'

'Right you are, dear. Have fun.'

I turned my phone screen to show Mum's photo to Robert. When he'd examined it more closely, he emitted a long, low whistle of admiration.

'That is a nice piece,' was his understatement. 'Send the photo to me, and I'll print a large colour copy to show Maudie and co. They'll find it a lot easier to see as a photographic enlargement than on a phone screen. Come on, we'll clear this lot up later.'

Leaving the array of dirty dishes and the debris from brunch on the breakfast bar, I followed him out of the room and down the corridor to his study that overlooked the back garden.

'While I fire up my computer, take a look at that little mirror-lined corner cabinet on the wall – home to my netsuke collection. You can open it up and take them out, if you like.'

As he pressed various buttons and his PC and printer whirred into life, I turned the tiny key in the door of the display cabinet to see more clearly the array of tiny carvings. Some were animals, such as a bullfrog licking a fly off its nose, and a curled, sleeping cat. Others were humanoid, such as a girl in a shift brushing her long hair and a gnarled old man in a loincloth and conical hat, smoking a pipe.

'The detail is exquisite,' I said, hardly daring to stroke the sleeping cat's fur for fear of damaging it. 'But I guess they had to be robust enough to serve their practical purpose, so maybe they're not as fragile as their delicacy suggests.'

'Indeed,' said Robert, loading a few sheets of glossy photographic paper into his printer.

'Our brown bear would make a fitting companion for this little lot,' I remarked.

Robert raised his eyebrows at me.

'Don't get too proprietorial about it yet,' he advised. 'Remember, it's gone missing. And if and when we do find it, our first action must be to take it to the police as evidence against Clive's murderer. Unless the killer was wearing gloves, which many of the Santas on the run had donned for warmth. Let's hope he—'

'Or she,' I put in.

'Or she, has left a useful set of fingerprints on our little teddy's fur.'

'How much more helpful if the carver had left the surface smooth rather than marking it with individual hairs. The texture might make a fingerprint harder to decipher.'

'But not DNA residue,' said Robert.

'Goodness,' I replied. 'And there was me thinking how tiny the bear was. Beside a DNA cell, it would be a monstrous giant.'

Robert chuckled. 'But before we do anything else, we must do our best to identify the carving's origin. Because if it turns out it is no ordinary button, but a rare and valuable antique – or at least that someone thought it was a rare and valuable antique – it could be a motive for murder. There might be some deranged collector out there who might kill in order to possess it.'

'We'd better not say that to Maudie and friends,' I replied. 'What reason can we give them for wanting to find it?'

Robert considered for a moment. 'That I was hoping to acquire it for my own netsuke collection?'

'That sounds as valid as any other explanation we might dream up.'

Robert picked the photos up from the tray of his printer and waved them about to ensure the ink was dry before slipping them in a protective, clear, plastic pocket.

'OK, then, let's go sleuthing. The sooner we can solve this case the better.'

He was right. We didn't want Clive's murder to cast a grim shadow over our first Christmas together, or to kill the festive spirit now taking hold of the village. But more importantly, justice must be done.

19

GOING ON A BEAR HUNT

'Actually, before we go grilling any of our three target ladies about the original ownership of the netsuke, how will it get us any further forward in our investigation of Clive's murder?' I wondered aloud as Robert set the burglar alarm just inside his front door.

'Good question.' He pulled the front door closed behind him and deadlocked it. 'I suppose there are several considerations. First, if the netsuke had been in the village for a long time, it would suggest that Clive might have a local connection that we didn't realise.'

'Like he might be related to Maudie or Mrs Jorkins or the vicar's wife, and trying to recover a family heirloom that he thought was rightfully his.'

'In that case, the murderer might be another relative involved in a family feud about ownership.'

'How bizarre to kill a relative, let alone a stranger, over such a tiny artefact,' I said. 'Even if it does turn out to be worth a large amount of money in relation to its size.'

'Or its value might be purely sentimental. Perhaps it was prised from the clutch of someone on their deathbed, their comforter in their final hours, and the rest of the family had wanted them to be buried with it. There have been stranger deathbed requests.'

'Or perhaps it's the missing piece of a set of netsuke owned by another relative, and the collection's value would be vastly increased if it was restored to its companion pieces.'

'Have they released Clive's surname into the public arena yet, or any other personal details?' asked Robert. 'If it's a local village name, like mine, that would be a handy clue.'

'I'd far rather it wasn't,' I admitted. 'I'd prefer not to have a murderous family in the midst of our community.'

Robert nodded. It was all right for him. He had a complex security system protecting his house. All I had at the Curiosity Shop was a biscuit tin painted to resemble a burglar alarm mounted above the front door.

'It'll be a dead giveaway, if you'll excuse the pun, if any of the three women we're questioning show any signs of grief for a sudden death in the family,' I observed. 'They must have been able to contact his next of kin by now.'

'"Twere well it were done quickly,' proclaimed Robert in dramatic tone. Then, abandoning all thoughts of *Macbeth*, he reverted to his normal gentle manner. 'Because the condition of the body isn't going to get any better the longer they leave it. Not until it's released for embalming, anyway, and I doubt they'll do that until they've found Clive's killer.'

I shuddered at that ghastly image, glad that we'd have to end the conversation there, having reached Maudie Frampton's house. I glanced at my watch. It was just gone eleven, so good timing regarding Sunday church and lunch habits. I rapped the door knocker, which had been fashioned from a discarded horse-shoe, and was now wrapped in a threadbare strand of tinsel as a token gesture at Christmas decoration.

'Mr Frampton's grandfather was village farrier,' explained Robert as I admired it.

Maudie answered the door.

'If it's my preserves you're after, they're all gone,' was her greeting. 'I sold clean out on my stall yesterday.'

She may have been characteristically grumpy, but she showed no sign of bereavement.

'So I heard, Maudie. I'm so pleased for you. Mum did well on her stall too.'

'Aye, I looked out for her, as it was her first time.'

To Maudie, Mum probably seemed young.

'That you, Maudie, that was very kind of you. She really appreciated your help. But we've come to ask you about something else.'

She narrowed her eyes.

'My button box?' she guessed. 'You changed your mind about it?'

Her telltale glance at her feet made me guess what she'd spent her button box money on: a neat pair of wide T-bar shoes with Velcro straps, the sort designed to accommodate old ladies' feet misshapen from a youth of squeezing into fashionable shoes and easily fastened by hands stiff with arthritis.

It was the first time I'd seen Maudie wearing a pair of proper ladies' shoes – or indeed any shoes the right size for her. Usually, she took turns at wearing her husband's hobnailed boots. She may well have been wearing her new shoes at the fair the day before, but I'd only seen her standing behind her stall, her feet invisible to passers-by. They could have been clad in shoe-boxes for all I knew.

She was probably worried that I wanted to return the button box for a refund.

'No, no, not at all,' I replied hastily. 'No, I'm very glad to have bought it from you. I've since bought similar ones from Mrs Jorkins and Mrs Shepherd too. It's just that after I'd sorted them all out by type, size, colour and so forth, Mum came across one that was really special, and now she can't find it.'

Perhaps realising I was starting to falter with my feeble attempt at lying, Robert picked up my thread.

'She'd really like to buy another similar one to replace it, so we were wondering whether you had any more like it tucked away anywhere.'

When he produced one of the photos of the bear netsuke from the plastic wallet, Maudie squinted at it inconclusively.

'I'll have to fetch my specs,' she announced, before heading back down the shadowy hallway.

'Someone selling something?' called the familiar rasping voice of Mr Frampton from within their little parlour.

'Buying, more like,' his wife called to him through the door, to be met with a disgruntled, 'Dearie me. Didn't oughta be trading on the Lord's day.'

I took advantage of Maudie's absence to congratulate Robert on coming up with such an innocent answer to her question.

A moment later, the bespectacled Maudie trudged back up the passage and took the photograph from Robert's outstretched hand. Stepping out onto the newly scrubbed doorstep for more light, she lifted her glasses up from the bridge of her nose to peer under them, then sighed with disappointment as she removed them, folded them up, and slipped them into the bulging pocket of her wraparound pinafore. I wondered what else lurked within.

'What is it, then, a little pussy cat? Some sort of dog? No, it's not one of mine. I'd have remembered if I'd had a button like that.'

'Actually, I think it's a bear,' I said.

'Never seen it before in me life, nor nothing like it,' she declared. 'Not that I didn't wish I never hadn't. It's quite a cute little thing. Oh!' She looked up from the picture. 'Would that be the one young Tilly was on about wanting at the Christmas fair? A button like a teddy bear?'

I nodded. I didn't want to say too much, for fear of making her connect it with the murder.

'Yes, that's right.'

'Well, I wish I did have another one to give her. But the thing is, I never even had that one in the first place, and that's the truth. I'm sorry to disappoint you.'

Robert slipped his free hand into his trouser pocket and pulled out half a dozen pound coins.

'Thank you all the same, Mrs Frampton, you've been most helpful. Here's a small thank-you for your trouble.'

When he slipped the coins into Maudie's outstretched hand, her eyes lit up.

'I'm not unhappy to help you, I'm sure,' she replied, still gazing at the coins in her open palm as she closed the door.

As we heard her trudging back down her hall, we heard her call loudly to her hard-of-hearing husband, 'Money for nothing don't count as selling, do it, Frampton?'

I grinned as we returned up the garden path to rejoin the high street.

'You've been reading too many old detective stories, Robert,' I teased him. 'Surely only the toffs in Sherlock Holmes or Lord Peter Wimsey mysteries give monetary tips to informers. And aren't their beneficiaries usually street urchins or reformed criminals?'

Robert slid a sly sideways smile at me. 'Call it noblesse oblige. But don't worry, I don't plan to insult the Jorkinses or Mrs Shepherd by crossing their palms with silver. The poor old Framptons are a special case.'

20

AS CHEERY AS FRESH PAINT

Although the Jorkinses lived in the same terrace as the Framptons, the difference in their fortunes was evident even as we opened the front garden gate. Whereas at the Framptons' the paint was blistering and the rusty hinges creaked, here the smartly painted gate swung soundlessly open onto an immaculately weeded gravelled path. From a nail on the front door hung a lush, thick wreath of glossy pine and holly branches dripping with shining red berries, and adorned with an inner circle of nut-brown pine cones secured with florist's wire. A huge bow of scarlet ribbon accentuated the glowing holly berries. Their front windows were festooned with fairy lights, but, doubtless to save on their electricity bill, they weren't yet turned on.

I rang the doorbell, a modern camera type, which gave the old couple the upper hand over whoever turned up on their doorstep.

'Ooh, young Alice and young Bobby!' cried Mrs Jorkins, her rosy apple cheeks glowing with delight when she opened the door to us. She can't have been much younger than Nell, the only other person whom I'd heard call Robert 'Bobby'. His more frequent village nickname was Bob Sponge, in honour of the invention that had made his fortune – the everlasting washing-up sponge. 'What can I do for you this fine crisp morning?'

Her warm welcome was so much more encouraging than Maudie's, lifting my spirits. Perhaps our quest wasn't so hopeless after all.

'Good morning, Mrs Jorkins,' replied Robert. 'We just wanted to ask you a quick question, if we may.'

I hoped he'd think to make his story consistent with what we had said to Maudie. These two old ladies, close in age and near neighbours, would be bound to exchange notes on their conversations with us.

'There was a particularly delightful button in the collections Alice bought from a few people in the village, and we've somehow mislaid it. But Alice's mum would love to source some more of the same, so we wanted to ask whether the original came from your collection, and if so, whether you had any more like it that you'd be willing to sell.'

'Of course, dear.' Mrs Jorkins wiped her hands on her apron, patterned with robins and reindeer. It must have been her special Christmas apron. I guessed we'd caught her in the process of preparing their traditional Sunday dinner. 'What did it look like? I knew every button in that tin like the freckles on the back of my hand, I played so much with it when I was a nipper. Some of the buttons had come off clothes my grandmother and all her brothers and sisters had worn as little ones. That's what they did in those days, see, wore their clothes into holes, and when there wasn't enough of the original left to hold another patch, they cut them up for rag rugs, and we salvaged the buttons to use again later. There weren't none of those charity shops you see about so much these days. There'd be a good jumble sale now and again, usually at start and end of winter, and otherwise they made do.'

She sounded rightly proud of her forebears' resourcefulness.

'They could teach us a thing or two about avoiding waste,' I said warmly. 'Do you know, I've never made a rag rug.'

'I'll teach you if you like,' said the old lady. 'One day when I've time to call me own, I'll stop by your shop and show you how it's done, just like my grandma taught me.'

My inner museum worker thrilled at the thought of receiving instruction that had been handed down so many generations.

With a tactful cough to bring us back on track, Robert produced the photo of the wooden bear from the plastic wallet again.

'This is the little fellow,' he told her, tapping the bear's nose.

She took the photo from him and held it at arm's length to focus.

'What a dear little soul. I can see why Mrs Carroll wants another. But I'm afraid I can be of no assistance there. I've some little animals on my mantelpiece, and one of those is a bear, but they wouldn't last five minutes as buttons, being made of china. Wade's Whimsies, they called 'em. We used to get them in Christmas crackers back in the day, and they were quite the thing for swapsies with your friends. You can't get 'em like that now, more's the pity.'

My face must have lit up. I had a few Wade's Whimsies in my shop already, and my mum had already filled me in on their background and their place in English domestic social history.

'But if I see any around, I'll be sure to tell you. Now, I must go, I can hear my taters starting to boil over, and I only want 'em parboiled to roast. Mr Jorkins is very partial to his roast potatoes of a Sunday.'

'Thank you very much, Mrs Jorkins.' I smiled. Seeing Mrs

Jorkins always makes me smile. 'And I'll take you up on your kind offer about rag rugs when you're ready. They'd be a great new line for my Curiosity Shop.'

'It'll be my pleasure, my dear, I'm sure,' she said, with a little wave that jangled the ancient silver charm bracelet on her wrist before she closed the door.

21

THE CLEANSING PROPERTIES OF DEATH

'Please don't tell me you want me to take those wretched buttons back again!' Mrs Shepherd, the vicar's wife, slumped against her front door jamb in an imitation of fainting. 'I thought I'd seen the last of those. I can't bear it.'

This was not a good start. As we'd approached the vicarage, I'd murmured to Robert, 'It feels a bit wrong to be disturbing the vicar's household on the Sabbath. Do you think we should come back tomorrow instead?'

Robert quickly dissuaded me with what seemed a logical argument.

'For a vicar, Sunday is by far his or her busiest working day. Mrs Shepherd would be much crosser if we came calling on a Monday, her husband's day of rest, when they probably want to keep themselves to themselves.'

Even so, I felt uncomfortable pressing the ancient china button on the vicarage front door, despite the word PRESS painted onto the enamel, reminding me of the EAT ME and DRINK ME labels in Alice's Adventures in Wonderland.

At first, I was glad Mrs Shepherd opened the door rather than the vicar. But her adverse reaction to our first mention of the word 'button' took me by surprise – and made me wonder whether she knew something about buttons that I didn't.

'I suppose you'd better come inside,' she said, straightening her back. 'Crispin wouldn't like me to be showing weakness on the doorstep.'

Robert and I exchanged anxious glances before accepting her invitation to follow through the echoing hallway, painted in a very pale blue, and into her sitting room where a tall, thin, sparsely decorated Christmas tree was already dropping pine needles onto the floor of the bay window. The colour scheme might have seemed cooling on a warm summer's day, but now in December it made it feel colder indoors than out.

This was my first time inside the vicarage, and I took advantage of the opportunity to observe what lay beyond the net curtains that masked its high-ceilinged rooms from curious passers-by. The tall bay sash windows must have required a lot of net to keep the vicar's activities secret. I hated to think how much the moth-eaten navy velvet curtains, now tied back with fading gold silk tassels, must have cost new.

Mrs Shepherd stepped forward to remove several large cardboard boxes occupying the old chintz sofa and armchairs. She took a seat in an armchair, while Robert and I tiptoed around stacks of books that covered the central rug, reminding me of the piles of tiles that support the floor of a Roman villa's hypocaust.

Mrs Shepherd sighed. 'You'll have to excuse the clutter. I'll conquer it eventually. I'm determined. If you ask my husband, he'll tell you I'm nothing if not determined. But we only have so many days on God's earth to achieve our aims, and every day that goes by without completing my task, I'm another day closer to the grave.'

'Oh goodness, I'm sorry, I didn't know you were unwell.' I

began to get to my feet, blushing our untimely intrusion, but Robert laid a hand on my forearm to keep me seated.

To my relief, Mrs Shepherd laughed and laughed, as if I'd made a hilarious joke. 'Oh, good Lord, I'm not ill. I'm not sick in any way, praise be. Living in the refrigerators that pass for vicarages for thirty years has hardened me against physical illness. Any germs that cling on to me when I'm out and about leap off and run the minute I enter my front door, driven by their instincts for self-preservation.'

She reached forward to pluck a book off the coffee table, just one of about a hundred teetering in crooked piles. 'No, I'm Swedish death cleaning.'

How very festive, I wanted to say, but didn't.

'It's the Swedish practice of minimising your possessions well before you expect to die, so as not to burden your children with the responsibility after your funeral. Or if you have to go into a care home, whichever comes quicker.' She waved her arms to encompass the various heaps all over the floor. 'Those buttons I offloaded onto you are just a tiny tip of the iceberg, Alice. All of this lot has to go.'

Robert and I gazed around the room, as she clearly expected us to do, in hope of garnering our sympathy.

'It's all very well for normal people around here,' she continued. 'They can just put anything they don't want into the next jumble sale, or, if it's decent stuff, sell it via your shop, Alice. But so much of what's here has been given to us over the years by parishioners, with the kindest intentions but seldom the best of taste, that if I want rid of it, I have to export it beyond the village for fear of offending the donors. Way beyond the village, to reach charity shops they're unlikely to frequent. Since Harvest Festival, I've been making weekly trips as far afield as Broadwick and even Highbere, ditching a car bootful at a time.'

I considered an array of old vases, lined up behind the Christmas tree on the wooden window seat as if about to face a firing squad.

'That's a shame,' I ventured. 'Some of the china vases there would make a great display in my shop. Plus I'd pay you, of course, if and when I sold them, unlike a charity shop or jumble sale.'

This was the trading tradition Nell had established when she ran the shop before me – a canny move as it enabled her to keep the shop fully stocked without tying up too much capital.

'No can do,' retorted Mrs Shepherd, getting up from her armchair and crossing to the window seat, where she stood, tapping each vase in turn, citing its donor – all names I knew from the village. When she reached a beautiful orange, yellow and black Clarice Cliff vase halfway along, she paused and turned to Robert.

'I'm sorry, Robert, you probably remember you and your dear late wife kindly gave us this little beauty for our silver wedding, but it doesn't match anything else in the house. Please know that we appreciated it very much on receipt. But you see the dilemma I'm in? If you'd like to take it home with you, please do, otherwise it's destined for a charity shop, I'm afraid.' I wondered why she was just giving so much stuff away. From the state of the interior décor of the vicarage, it looked as if she needed the money. 'Any flowers in the house will be in plain jam jars or milk jugs from now on. People always look at the flowers, anyway, not the receptacle holding them.'

A shadow crossed Robert's face as he took the proffered vase from her and wrapped both arms around it. He swallowed.

'I know you appreciated the spirit in which we gave it to you,' he said at last. 'And I shall think of you and Mr Shepherd every time I use it.'

No doubt he'd be thinking of his late wife too. But I liked that Robert, even as a man living by himself, habitually filled his house with fresh flowers, even at this time of year. I marvelled at his ability to keep poinsettias alive, an art I'd never managed to master.

'So you can see why, Alice, you were doing me a favour by taking that old button box off my hands. If I come across anything else that I want to dispose of that doesn't have its origins with kind parishioners, I hope I may bring them to you for your shop. It would be so much easier than trekking back and forth to various market towns.'

'Of course,' I said quickly, still slightly discombobulated by her mentioning Robert's late wife. Perhaps Mrs Shepherd didn't know Robert and I were sort of dating. Perhaps she didn't approve.

Only when Robert drew the photograph of the netsuke bear out of his plastic wallet did I refocus on the purpose of our visit.

'Just one thing, if you don't mind, before we leave you to your sorting,' he said. 'Can you tell us whether this little wooden toggle might have come from your button box?'

When he passed the picture to her for closer inspection, she frowned.

'Doesn't look like a toggle to me. More of a kids' toy, or perhaps some kind of souvenir from a zoo, or a lucky mascot. I'm sure it didn't come from my button box. If it had been, I'd have taken it out and put it in the sack of my children's disused toys.'

She pointed to a large plastic bag in the corner, from which protruded the long neck of a cuddly plush giraffe, apparently surveying the scene.

'Thanks very much, Mrs Shepherd, that's all we wanted to ask,' said Robert, slipping the photo back into its protective wallet. 'Sorry to have disturbed you on a Sunday.'

'Oh, don't mind me,' she replied, with a dismissive wave of her hand. 'I'm just glad to be distracted from this chaos for five minutes. Crispin's been out all day, first at morning service, then taking communion to the housebound, and now he's off to lunch at the bishop's manse and staying for evensong at the cathedral. Sundays can be surprisingly solitary for a vicar's wife, even for one who goes to all his parish services. I see even less of him in the run-up to Christmas.'

I was softening towards her. I'd previously assumed all vicars' spouses were towers of strength to their husband or wife, and a comfort to the parishioners too. Yet here she was, hale and hearty and, may I say, in her prime, already contemplating and preparing for the end of her life. I felt bad now that I'd never really spoken to her before, not being a churchgoer myself.

'Well, if you ever need a second opinion on any of the items you're disposing of, feel free to call in at my shop and we can discuss it over a cup of coffee. On the house, of course,' I added, realising that living on a vicar's stipend, going out to coffee might not be within her budget.

For the first time since our arrival, she smiled. 'I'd like that, Alice. I'd like that very much.'

When she reached out to shake our hands before she showed us out – something she hadn't done on our arrival – her thin fingers felt like so many frozen runner beans.

Just before she closed the door, I noticed a small, hard-shaped bulge in the front pocket of her skirt – the right size for a piece of netsuke.

22

TRANSFERENCE THEORY

'Why do you think Mrs Shepherd seemed so driven by the notion of Swedish death cleaning?' I asked Robert as we made our way back up the high street to his house. 'You don't think she has a feeling of impending doom, do you? Some kind of intimations of her own mortality that are making her panic?'

He shrugged. 'She looked perfectly healthy to me, although possibly in need of a good Sunday dinner with a proper pudding. Not that all illnesses are visible to the naked eye.'

'OK, perhaps not of her own mortality, but of an impending loss of freedom that's making her want to set her affairs in good order?'

Robert gave me a sideways look. 'What, you mean as if she's about to be found guilty of some misdemeanour that will send her to prison?'

I nodded. 'I couldn't have put it better myself.'

The corners of his lips twitched as he tried to suppress a smile. 'And on what evidence exactly do you suspect her of Clive's murder?'

I bit my lip. He'd rumbled me. 'I suppose I am jumping the

gun a bit. But just think, Robert, what if she had stolen a highly valuable netsuke from Clive, planning to sell it to supplement her husband's modest income? This extreme decluttering could be a front. A tiny wooden carving might easily be stashed away among all the stuff until she had a chance to sell it. In fact, just as we were leaving, I noticed a bump in her skirt pocket that could easily have been a small wooden carving. And what about these trips to charity shops and antique dealers in towns where no one knows her? They could be a decoy for meeting a fence to sell stolen valuables on the black market.'

'Now who's been watching too many detective films?' He grinned. 'And where does Santa Clive come into this scenario?'

I thought for a moment. 'Perhaps he was her brother, and he was going to steal it on her behalf so no one would suspect her. You must admit a Santa suit on the day of a Santa Run is a clever disguise – easy to organise, and the perfect camouflage.'

'But why would Mrs Shepherd then strangle her own brother with the green scarf before running off with the netsuke?' asked Robert. 'Why rip it off the scarf at all, when it would be much less conspicuous left sewn onto the scarf?'

'Because everyone would be looking for the green scarf, as in their eyes, what had been stolen was the scarf, and that was the crime they wanted restitution for. Only when we discovered the bear was missing from the abandoned scarf did we realise the real motivation for the theft – and attempted murder – even though the police don't seem to believe us.'

'That still doesn't explain why she'd kill her own brother,' Robert said.

'Let's not forget I'm only speculating on that being the nature of their relationship. Do we know anything of Mrs Shepherd's past? Clive might have been an ex-lover, spurned in her youth, who had returned in the hope of a mid-life reunion. Or he might be an ex-convict that her evidence had sent to jail years ago, and having just been released, he was bent on revenge. Or perhaps he was a current lover, threatening to expose their relationship to her husband and children. If only we knew her maiden name, we could check out the blood tie theory straight away. That's got to be the easiest one to prove or disprove.'

'Oh, but I do,' said Robert. 'You see, she's my friend Matthew's younger sister. I know her family well, and as far as I'm aware, there's not a Clive among them.'

The mounting excitement I'd felt while propounding my theories lay shattered like a crystal glass dropped on a flagstone floor.

'Perhaps we'd better take a step or two backwards,' Robert suggested. 'Let's not jump to any more conclusions about anybody involved, until we can identify a clear motive. In the meantime, we'd better turn over the last unexplored avenue that might tell us the origin of the netsuke bear.'

I looked at him blankly.

'Nell Little,' he continued. 'Isn't there at least a chance that the bear was originally part of Nell's stock when you bought the shop, and she'd just shoved it in a button box thinking it was a novelty button?'

It was the simplest and most obvious solution. I kicked myself for not thinking of that before we'd bothered Maudie Frampton, Mrs Jorkins and Mrs Shepherd.

'Once we know its origins for sure, we'll have a better idea of its true value – and whether that's enough for anyone to be prepared to kill in order to possess it.'

I sighed. 'Of course. When I started sorting the various button boxes out, including the one in Nell's original stock, I found all sorts of things that shouldn't have been in there – an old shopping list, an odd earring, a small penknife. It would be so easy for things to get hidden there. I even lost my wristwatch to a tin of buttons for a little while. I'd taken it off and set it on the counter the afternoon Martin came to visit, while I was in the middle of sorting them, and I swept it into one of the tins, along with the buttons scattered across the counter.'

'That's agreed, then. Next stop, Nell's care home, to ask whether she recognises the carving.'

'What a fool I'll look if Nell tells me it's a valuable piece she'd had in stock for ages, that no one had ever been prepared to pay her asking price for – and I'd just treated it as almost worthless.'

Robert glanced at his watch. 'Let's restore ourselves with a cup of coffee before we set off for Wendlebury Barrow. Then we should get to Nell's care home just after she's had her Sunday lunch.'

'Goodness, is it that time already?'

With all our comings and goings, I'd rather lost track.

'Only in the care home's time zone. They have a policy of early rising, so by midday, the residents are ready for their lunch. I tell you what, in the interests of supporting local traders, why don't we jump in the car now and have our coffee at the tea room in Hector's House, instead of at your place or mine? Let someone else wait on us for a change. We need to save our energies for getting to the bottom of Clive's murder.'

I couldn't have agreed more.

23

ELEVENSES AT TWELVE

'Goodness, how Tilly's grown,' exclaimed the languid curly-haired fellow perching on a stool behind the bookshop's trade counter. He was wearing a black T-shirt lettered in orange, *Books make the best presents.* 'Children grow up so fast these days, don't they?'

Robert gave a good-natured chuckle. 'OK, Hector, I take your point. I haven't brought Tilly here for ages. But I will do soon. I promised to take her Christmas shopping, provided she bought all her little friends books instead of toys. They'll all have quite enough toys from their families, and you can never have too many books, can you?'

Hector, who I gathered from his name to be the bookshop's proprietor, could hardly disagree with that statement. 'I've a wish-list here from all the primary school teachers round about, in case she needs to buy her class teacher a gift too. But sorry, I'm homing in on sales opportunities, rather than the identity of your charming companion.'

Pot, kettle, I thought. I'd not said a word to him yet, but he was already winning me over.

'Alice Carroll,' I said. 'Of Alice's Cotswold Curiosity Shop in Little Pride, so a fellow local trader. Pleased to meet you.'

Hector raised a forefinger as if he'd just seen the light. 'Ah, yes, the new Nell Littlewood. A pleasure to meet you too. I hope you're going to continue Nell's policy of giving me first pick of any old books that come your way for my second-hand department upstairs. I promise I'll give you a good price for them.'

'Fine by me,' I replied. 'We've just come for coffee today, before we go to visit Nell up the high street at the care home, but we must have a proper chat about business soon. Perhaps when I come back for a bit of Christmas shopping myself. I really must make a start on it.'

'I'm sure Sophie will take very good care of you in the meantime.'

At the sound of her name, a tall girl in her late twenties with tinsel in her hair set down the bowl of sugar she was just topping up at one of the café tables, and beckoned us to the last empty table in the tea room at the back of the bookshop.

Once she had persuaded us to forego the coffee in favour of some fancy hot chocolates topped with whipped cream and gingerbread stars, I pulled a notebook and pen from my handbag and began to write another checklist.

1. *Ask Nell if the bear was hers or whether she knows anyone else locally who might source such things, e.g. a local netsuke collector.*

2. *If yes, ask her to estimate its value so we know whether it was worth stealing – and (shudder) killing for.*

3. *Go online to find out all we can about Clive's identity – origin, occupation, etc – that might tell us his motive for the theft.*

I looked up at Robert before adding point four.

'Do you realise we've made another rookie error here?' I asked him. 'Apart from not starting with Nell.'

His brow furrowed. 'Tell me.'

'We never actually looked for the bear in the rec. We were so intent on getting Clive the medical attention he needed, and on making sure the news of his assault didn't spoil the fair, that we didn't think to do a fingertip search of the field. Supposing the little bear has just been lying there unnoticed all this time? And that when we find him, he turns out to be a mass-produced plastic toy, or some other worthless piece of junk that Mum sewed on for fun? We have only Mum's word to go on that it was hand-carved from wood. And Tilly's, of course. But she values her Sylvanians and her Barbies as much as if they were solid gold.'

Robert licked the whipped cream from his gingerbread star and put it on his saucer. 'You're forgetting Wendy's photograph of the scarf that Jack put on Facebook. The bear doesn't look like cheap plastic junk on there.'

I pulled out my phone and navigated to my gallery to find the picture Mum had also sent to me. I zoomed in on the bear and turned the screen to face Robert.

'It does look pretty special, probably vintage if not antique,' I remarked. 'Even at this screen resolution, which is quite low, you can see the individual hairs carved into the bear's coat. And if that's the case, what's the betting its green eyes aren't coloured glass or plastic, but some kind of precious gemstone?'

'You're right,' said Robert. 'I think we should assume it's a valuable antique netsuke, worth pinching, unless and until proven otherwise. It could be that the person who took it from Clive didn't mean to kill him, but only to incapacitate him for long enough to rip the bear off the scarf and run away.'

'If only Clive had realised, perhaps he could have just handed over the scarf, bear and all. Resisting might have signed his own death warrant.'

When I noticed the buzz of chatter around the room had halted, and everyone's eyes were turned in my direction, I realised how ghoulish our conversation would sound out of context.

'But apart from that it was a great film,' Robert improvised cleverly, and everyone turned back to their own business.

Sophie made eye contact with me as she cleared empty coffee cups from the adjacent table.

'Did I hear you say "netsuke"?' she asked brightly. 'By chance, we've just got a huge and lovely hardback into stock about Japonisme, the nineteenth-century trend for all things Japanese and its influence on Western art. Plus there's a copy of Edmund de Waal's memoir about the netsuke collection passed down through his family, *The Hare with Amber Eyes*. If you're having a bit of belated Japonisme yourselves, they're both worth reading. The art book would make a great Christmas present.' With a mischievous glint in her eyes, she looked at each of us in turn. 'Only make sure you don't both buy a copy for each other, or you'll have swaps.'

I smiled politely, still anxious about the prospect of exchanging Christmas gifts with Robert. A nice coffee-table book would be great in return for the jumper I was already secretly knitting for him, or even the paperback memoir, but I'd been hoping for something more personal and romantic than a book.

'Actually, I've already got Robert's gift lined up, but thanks for the suggestion,' I told her.

At least now Robert knew that I was getting him something, so I should avoid the embarrassment of presenting him with a gift only to find he had bought nothing for me.

'I'll be back,' Robert told Sophie in his best Arnold Schwarzenegger impression. 'But for now, Alice and I had better be off to see Nell before her post-prandial snooze.'

As we left the shop, he added to me, 'That should just about give us time before it gets dark to comb the rec for our little ursine friend.'

'Eh?' I blinked.

'That which pertains to bears,' he translated.

'Ah,' I said. 'Now you're speaking my language.'

24

NELL AND NETSUKE

'Bit of an odd coincidence, isn't it, that Hector's House should stock not one but two books that might help us in our investigation,' said Robert as we strolled the length of the pleasant high street to the Manor House Care Home, where Nell now lived.

The whole village of Wendlebury Barrow, with its low stone cottages the colour of set honey, felt like a home from home after six months of living in Little Pride. Here too the neat rows of old houses were interrupted now and again by a larger, more ostentatious one, probably once home to a rich medieval wool merchant. Most front doors were adorned with lavish festive wreaths, and despite the daylight, some households had already turned on their Christmas lights. At the other end of the architectural scale, a handful of modern homes plugged gaps that must once have been paddocks, like the plot next to the Curiosity Shop.

Robert patted the book bag under his arm. Hector, picking up on Sophie's comments, had sought out the two books, displayed alluringly on oak bookstands on the trade counter. Grinning at the hint, Robert had bought them both, plus a branded hessian bag to carry them in.

'Maybe someone local with an interest in netsuke ordered them in for their own research,' I speculated.

'You mean Clive, or his attacker? Could be. Anyway, they're ours now.'

I was glad of that, especially as they weren't now going to be my Christmas present.

'Besides, I wouldn't mind a cosy evening reading by the fire together after our exertions of the day, a glass of something warming in hand,' Robert continued as we arrived at Nell's.

Our timing was perfect. Nell's empty lunch tray was still on the table in front of her chair, and she was enjoying a cup of tea. I detected from the traces on her plate that she'd enjoyed a homely meal of shepherd's pie and greens, followed by a dark fruit crumble – cherry, or perhaps apple and blackberry – with custard. It was good to see she was being well looked after.

I was glad to see lots of colourful streamers brightening every room, including Nell's. We'd even passed a post box for letters to Santa in reception.

Nell smiled as we approached, waving us towards the window seat, which was just wide enough for two people, provided they didn't mind being up close to each other.

'Young Bobby, my dear, and Alice. To what do I owe this lovely surprise?'

I felt bad now to have to confess we had a selfish reason for our visit. I made a mental note to pop in again before Christmas simply for a social call, and to bring her a Christmas card and a tin of toffees as her present. In my experience, old ladies love toffees, especially once they've lost all their teeth so don't have to worry about pulling out any fillings. Growing old isn't all bad, I've come to realise, as I age myself – although, I hasten to add, my teeth are all still my own.

Before joining me on the window seat, Robert stooped to kiss Nell's powdery cheek. He'd known her since he was a little boy, which was what she still thought of him as.

'Any more mysteries for me to help you solve?' she asked eagerly. 'I was glad to be of help to you with those other funny businesses. Makes me feel like a useful member of society instead of just sitting here having fun all day.'

She pointed a finger crooked with arthritis towards her bedside table, piled high with Christmas classics from the care home library, beside her current knitting project, a dusky pink bedjacket.

'Eating food someone else has prepared for you is always a treat, but it's my books and my knitting that keep my brain busy.'

'Actually, there is,' I began. 'And you are exactly the person we need to speak to about it.'

Brightening, she sat up a little straighter. 'Do tell!'

As happy as she was in her care home, she clearly relished the opportunity to be involved in something beyond her daily routine.

I explained our dilemma as delicately as I could, sparing the more grisly details of Clive's fatal injury, and stressing the importance of the bear. At the appropriate moments, Robert pulled out his enlarged print of the bear, now a little creased at the corners, to show her exactly what it looked like.

Nell put a forefinger to her lip before she spoke.

'What a beauty!' she declared. 'A fine piece of knitting, very even, in linen stitch, if I'm not mistaken?'

'The knitting's by my mum,' I told her. 'But we don't know where the little wooden bear came from. You see, I gave Mum free access to all the buttons in my shop to decorate the things she'd knitted for the Christmas fair. The buttons had recently been brought in by three different ladies in the village, but none of them recognised it. Therefore, we wondered whether it was old stock from your time.'

Nell shook her head. 'I wish it was. I love bears of all kinds. If I'd had it, I'd have kept it and brought it in here as a little friend to join my others.'

She pointed to a neat row of tiny china, wooden and metal bears on one of the bookshelves in the alcove opposite her bed. All were lined up to face her. I wondered if she had conversations with them when no one else was in the room. She must have missed the daily companionship of her customers.

'Then I can only assume I missed it when I was combining and sorting the various boxes of buttons,' I concluded. 'I still can't quite believe it, as even among the decorative vintage ones from Maudie Frampton and Mrs Jorkins, it would have stood out.' I tapped the sparkling gemstones in the photo. 'For a start, buttons don't usually have eyes. And it's so much more substantial than the other buttons – quite three-dimensional.'

'Maybe you didn't miss it, my dear,' Nell said gently. 'Maybe when you looked, it wasn't there. Perhaps your mother brought it in her knitting bag from home, and it was never part of the shop stock at all?'

I shook my head. 'Absolutely. I've asked her. Mum swears she found it in one of my button boxes.'

'Then there's only one sensible conclusion,' said Nell. 'Someone must have put it there between you sorting the button boxes and your mother choosing which buttons to use. But who would do such a thing, and why?'

I extracted my notebook from my handbag and added Nell's question to my list.

'That's remarkable,' I said, as I put the cap back on my pen.

'Even though you're tucked away in here, you still see things I've missed.'

Nell's eyes lit up. 'So I haven't outlived my usefulness yet, my dear. And now, in return for my surmise, you can tell me about all the things in the village that I am so missing, especially at this time of year. How is my shop – your shop – doing just now? And Suki Price and Coralie and Mrs Frampton and the Jorkinses? How is the dear vicar? Not too rushed off his feet, I hope. Who was the fastest in the Santa Run this year? And how big is the Christmas tree on the village green? I hope it's a straighter spec-imen than last year's, which was proper wonky.' She shot a longing glance at her bedside table. 'Before we start, be so good as to pass me my knitting. I'm getting close to finishing the second sleeve today. I'm quite excited about it.'

Hoping she didn't notice Robert checking his watch, I answered her questions as succinctly as possible while she clicked away with her knitting needles. It was important to get back to Little Pride before dark, so that we could search for the bear in the rec, just in case it was still there. Although it seemed unlikely, if anyone was going to find it, I wanted that anyone to be us.

25

ANOTHER BEAR HUNT

'You know, in a funny way, I feel a little envious of Nell's lifestyle,' I told Robert as he drove us back to Little Pride. 'All her meals cooked and brought to her on a tray, all her laundry done, no unwanted intrusions from the outside world, just her hobbies to look forward to each day.'

Robert raised his eyebrows. 'But if she had your youth, health and fitness, don't you think she'd swap with you in a flash? After being at the hub of the village most of her life, she must miss the buzz. Although lots of people visit her still, it won't be the same as having them en masse in her shop, or meeting them at village events.'

Chastened, I determined to make the most of every day I had in Little Pride, and not to take a single moment for granted.

'Shame we can't move the mountain to Mohammed,' I mused. 'Anyway, I'm impressed that she's still been able to help us, even without leaving her care home. Now we should just about have enough light left to search the rec for the bear. Talk about looking for a needle in a haystack: a small brown piece of wood in a sea of mud.'

Much of the grass in the rec had been transformed by the many sprinting Santas into bare, slippery soil.

'That may be so, but the last of the evening sun might be reflected in its glassy eyes to catch our attention.'

That was a bit optimistic. The sky was an unbroken leaden grey.

Robert slowed down as we approached the 30mph sign at the edge of the village. 'Maybe we should leave it until tomorrow, and go out in the brighter morning light?'

I checked the weather forecast on my phone.

'Torrential rain all day,' I reported gloomily. 'Not a sunbeam in sight!'

'Then I tell you what,' he said, pressing the button on his key fob to open the automatic gates to his drive. 'Why don't we have a late lunch now, and go to the rec after dark armed with torches? It might be easier to find the bear that way. Its gemstone eyes should reflect the torchlight like a cat's eyes.'

'You mean the type of cat's eye in the middle of the road or the kind on an actual cat?'

'Same difference,' said Robert, pulling on the handbrake and switching off the engine. 'Now, let me rustle us up a nice hot bowl of soup to fortify ourselves in the meantime.'

Even full of hot tomato soup, we had no luck with our torchlight investigations an hour later. We had a few moments of breathless excitement when our torch beams met with a reflection, but each time we were disappointed to find only ring-pulls from drink cans or scrunched-up silver foil sandwich wrappers dropped by picnickers who ignored the Countryside Code: take only photographs and leave only footprints. Either that or a couple of neighbourhood cats sneaking about in hope of the feline equivalent of a takeaway – a small, wild, nocturnal mammal.

With cold, damp feet and icy fingers, we were glad to return to the solid ground of the high street's pavement and the soft orange glow of the streetlamps and the twinkle of fairy lights in almost every house we passed to light our way home. It was only half past five, but it felt so much later. It had been a long, intense day.

'I really ought to be getting back to Mum now,' I said, reluctant to part from my companion when we reached his front gate. 'Having left her on her own in the shop all day, I'm feeling guilty of neglect. I'd better go and cook her tea, or at least eat it with her if she wants to cook. I'm afraid I'll have to take a raincheck on that fireside reading session with you.'

'Then you must take one of the books we bought home with you,' he insisted. 'These books won't read themselves, you know, and they might teach us something crucial about netsuke. Frankly, at the rate we're going, we need all the help we can get.'

I followed him into his house just long enough to choose which book to read. I chose the Edmund de Waal memoir, a more compact and portable volume to curl up with. Actually, I lingered a little longer – just long enough to exchange a kiss so warming that as I trudged back to the Curiosity Shop, every part of my body was tingling.

26

CATCHING UP WITH DANNY

By the time I got home, it was way past Sunday closing time for my shop, and Mum, bless her, had already cashed up and got stuck into cooking our tea in the kitchen. As I strolled through the dark shop, I could hear a man's voice coming from the living quarters beyond. After wondering for a split second whether Mum had either an intruder or a beau, I realised it was Danny.

'Hi, Alice, I've left Jack in peace to do his lesson preparation, and just popped back to see whether there were any developments about poor Clive.'

He took a sip from the mug of tea Mum had made him, while Mum flicked the switch on the kettle to make another one for me. She had a teabag at the ready in my favourite mug.

'Have you been all this time visiting those old lady friends, dear?' she asked. 'You must have worn the poor souls out.'

I may be fifty, but Mum still liked to know my whereabouts.

'Sorry, Mum, I should have messaged you to let you know we'd be back later than I'd originally estimated. The reason we took longer is that we waited until dark to search by torchlight for the bear in the rec.'

'Wouldn't it have been easier to look for him by day?' said Mum, tipping the sizzling contents of a saucepan into a casserole dish and slipping it into the oven.

'But less romantic,' said Danny, with a grin.

'That's not at all the point,' I said quickly. 'You see, we were working on the cat's eye principle. We thought it would be easier to spot the reflection of its gemstone eyes than to find a tiny brown piece of wood in a sea of mud in daylight. That would have been like looking for a specific piece of hay in a haystack.'

'And did you find it?' Danny pressed me.

Mum filled my mug from the reboiled kettle.

I gave a sheepish grin. 'No, but we did find some actual cats' eyes, complete with cats.'

'Still, it was a good idea to look for it,' said Danny. 'Why did none of us think of that before? Just because the bear was missing from the scarf used to assault Clive doesn't mean that stealing the bear was his attacker's motive. He might just have wanted to give Clive a fright – or worse.'

'Got it in one,' I said, adding milk to my mug from the jug on the table.

'But whatever his motive, if the thief dropped it as he fled the scene, the last thing we want is for some toddler to pick it up and take it home to play with, or for a dog off the lead to pick it up and eat and destroy the evidence. Dogs eat the strangest things.'

I grimaced.

'To be honest, Robert and I didn't think of it,' I replied. 'We were acting on Nell's suggestion.'

'She sounds like a remarkable old lady,' said Mum, coming to join us at the table, bringing a small glass of cooking sherry with her. Actually, it was Harveys Bristol Cream, but Dad and I always jokingly referred to it as Mum's cooking sherry because she always had a little glass of it while cooking our tea. 'I'd like to meet her some time.'

That surprised me. It is always disconcerting when two separate parts of your life collide, but now I realised Mum and Nell might rather get on. Plus, Nell would always welcome an additional visitor.

'So, how are you and Jack after the various events of Saturday?' I asked Danny. 'No coughs or colds after getting so wet and muddy yesterday? Or so stressed?'

Danny wrapped both hands around his mug of tea.

'No, just rather shaken up about poor Clive. We've been trying not to think of it, to be honest. Jack has plenty of end-of-term Christmassy stuff at school to distract him, such as the nativity play and the carol service and the whole-school outing to the pantomime in Broadwick. and I've been writing job applications today to take my mind off it.'

'Really?' This was a new development. He'd seemed a little reluctant to confront the possibility of redundancy last time we'd spoken about it. 'Are you sure this is a good time, in the run-up to Christmas? I'd have thought most employers would be too demob-happy to think about recruitment until the holiday season's over. Have you managed to find any suitable vacancies yet?'

Danny took a few sips of tea before replying. I suspected he was trying to think of the best way to tell me something I'd rather not hear. 'A couple in London, which would be a terrific step up career-wise, but disruptive to my personal life. They'd mean either an exhausting and expensive commute by train, or upping sticks and moving to the Big Smoke. Plus a couple elsewhere.'

My face fell. Perhaps he and Jack were not as close as I'd hoped.

'I see.' I tried not to sound as disappointed as I felt. If London life was what he wanted, he should go for it. Ten years younger than me, his career was still on an upward trajectory. Since I'd sidestepped into my shop and prioritised independence over wage-slavery – more by luck than judgement, I confess – I'd been far happier than I'd thought possible.

'Well, best of luck with all of those, Danny.' I forced the words out although they stuck in my throat. 'I wish you every success.'

27

AN INSIGHT FROM MUM

'You know there's still one person you haven't asked about that little bear's origins,' said Mum, as later we sat by the fire with our knitting. I'd reached the armholes of the back of Robert's Christmas present. 'And that's Coralie.'

I dropped a stitch at her unexpected suggestion.

'Coralie?' I held my work closer to my eyes to pick up the dropped stitch. 'Why Coralie? She didn't give me any buttons. It was the other way around. I only gave some to her. And the bear can't have been in that batch, because it was still here for you to find.'

'Oh yes, of course,' said Mum. 'I remember you telling me now. And then those naughty children broke into her little house and threw them all about. Not enough discipline from their parents, if you ask me. They probably get away with leaving their bedrooms all untidy at home. Did you ever find out which children did it?'

I let my knitting needles drop into my lap. 'Actually, Mum, we didn't. And we didn't have any proof it was children. That's just how she explained it away at the time. Nothing was stolen, and we couldn't think of any other reason for their intrusion except boredom or vengeance for a bad haircut. Besides, it's not as if they truly ransacked her tiny house. They didn't go around emptying out drawers or throwing foodstuffs about. All they did was chuck the buttons on the floor. I reckon once they'd done that, they realised how naughty they'd been and legged it before anyone could catch them.'

Despite my explanation, I was overwhelmed by my stupidity. By dismissing the raid on Coralie's tiny house, I'd just been believing what we wanted to believe: that I was not in any way to blame. Yet I'd indirectly pointed a stranger enquiring about buttons in her direction. Admittedly I'd only given him her Etsy shop details, but it wouldn't be Mission: Impossible to extrapolate her postal address.

Mum had stopped knitting, and was gazing at me as if waiting for me to catch on.

'So what that means is you have no proof that the vandal might not have been the very same person who'd come to your shop, asking to see your buttons.' She paused, putting her hand to her heart as if to calm its rapid beating. 'Goodness, it could have been so much worse.'

She covered her eyes with her hands as if trying to unsee a vision of me lying dead on the floor of my shop, buttons scattered around me and a buttonhook piercing my heart.

Her anguish was infectious. Supposing Coralie hadn't been playing skittles at the pub that night and the would-be thief had found her at home? If it was the same person who'd attacked Clive, he was the type who wouldn't stop short of murder. I felt a chill run through me as I pictured Coralie tumbling down the wooden steps of her tiny house, strangled with one of her button necklaces.

'But who would have known I had the netsuke in among my

buttons, if I didn't, Nell didn't, and nor did any of my button donors? And why all this fuss over a single piece of netsuke? I know the finer antique ones can change hands for thousands, but they're hardly priceless. We're not talking about an audacious heist of high art. It's hardly lifting the *Mona Lisa* from the Louvre.'

'Maybe it had value in other terms than money,' said Mum. 'Like the sentimental value of my great-grandmother's white china dogs that now live on my mantelpiece. They wouldn't make it onto *Antiques Roadshow*, but I wouldn't part with them for anything.'

It was true. Their worth was measured in a different currency. Every Easter, for as long as I can remember, Mum has tied fresh yellow ribbons around the china dogs' necks.

'Is it possible that someone would commit murder to regain possession of something purely for its sentimental value?' I asked.

I left the question hanging in the air. Without knowing the culprit and his or her state of mind, it was impossible to answer.

We both fell to thinking in silence as we resumed our knitting. Knitting's like that – it frees your mind to roam, while the soothing, repetitive action keeps your brain ticking over at a steady pace.

After a little longer, Mum finished a row, stabbed the points of her needles into the ball of snow-white yarn she was working with, and pushed herself up out of the armchair.

'I think I'll just pop upstairs and take a hot bath before bed, if that's OK,' she said.

When did my mother start asking my permission to do things?

'Fine, Mum, I'll stay down here a bit longer and have a quiet read,' I told her. 'I'm going to read this book about netsuke that we bought in the Wendlebury Barrow bookshop this afternoon.

Although I had promised myself not to start another book until I've finished that chess manual.'

'What a lovely extra Christmas present that would be for Robert if you told him you'd just learned to play chess especially for him,' said Mum, clasping her hands in front of her chest. 'Think of all those long romantic evenings it would spell, playing chess by the fire together, or in the summer in the garden.'

That was the most persuasive argument in favour of learning chess that I'd ever heard. As she made her way upstairs, I opened *Chess for Simpletons* once more.

28

THE UNFOLDING EVIDENCE

Chess for Simpletons fell open at the most viewed page – the introduction, which by then I'd read so often that I could practically recite it.

After reading it yet again, I plucked my bookmark out of the way of the first proper chapter – a bookmark that in the whirlwind of recent events I'd completely forgotten.

Japan comes to Highbere Museum

The font of the headline looked oriental, as if the designer had hoped to fool us into thinking we were reading actual Japanese.

I checked the dates of the special exhibition of Japonisme, the name given to the influence of Japanese art on European. It was to run until the end of February, bringing together original ancient Japanese artworks with the subsequent European response. The show included calligraphy and drawing, woodblock prints and paintings, textiles and fashion, pottery and sculpture, all displayed with interpretive labels to explain the vast and lasting impact of East meeting West in the middle of the nineteenth century.

I unfolded the flyer. *Six pages gatefold*, commented some dormant part of my brain. My job at Broadwick City Museum had occasionally involved producing similar publicity leaflets, only on a much lower budget than this thick, glossy paper suggested.

My interest in learning more was piqued by Highbere Museum's colourful brochure. I turned to the back page to view the map labelled *How to Find Us*, and I knew at once that we should visit. It could only help our investigation – especially when I spotted a photograph in the bottom right-hand corner of a small, dark, wooden bear with glinting green eyes.

It was startlingly familiar. No, it couldn't possibly be the one that Mum had sewn on the green scarf, although it looked very like it. No way could a museum piece have found its way into Mum's knitting supplies. The bear's pose and texture, with hair-like indents all over, did look very much like it, but it didn't mean it was the same one. Bears are bear-like, and perhaps one small carving of a bear in the same wood would look very much like another. Perhaps there'd been a Japanese carver who mass-produced the same design, and these little bears were commonplace.

Or perhaps Mum's bear was a cheap but faithful imitation of the original, made in response to the popularity of the original – the one now temporarily housed in Highbere Museum. You could buy copies of classic netsuke for thirty or forty quid these days. We'd even had a couple in the Broadwick City Museum shop during our exhibition of Japanese prints. They were probably also selling some in the Highbere Museum shop.

I stared at the photo for a while. Maybe I needed to see the original in three dimensions, and at close-up, to judge properly.

That need now felt urgent. Could I bunk off from the shop next day and head to Highbere Musuem?

I could easily ask Mum to mind the shop for another day in my absence. If I didn't go, she'd probably want to spend the day in the shop with me anyway. She liked keeping me company there, knitting away in the pale green Lloyd Loom chair that she seemed to have adopted as her own. She was probably secretly hoping no one would buy it and displace her, and I made a mental note to replace the price tag with a *Not for Sale* sign.

I was glad to have the excuse to visit the museum with Robert. I hadn't yet been to a museum with him, and I thought he'd enjoy that sort of thing, provided no one recognised him and tried to tap him for a hefty donation, or pressed him to join the board of trustees. I supposed he got that sort of pressure all the time.

I slipped the leaflet into my handbag and snapped *Chess for Simpletons* shut. It was time to get stuck into the Edmund de Waal memoir instead.

29

LOCAL INTELLIGENCE

'Alice, have you seen the local news on breakfast television?'

I hadn't put Robert down as a breakfast television viewer. Even so, I was glad to have a phone call from him before I opened the shop the next morning.

'Good morning to you too, Robert,' I said.

'Sorry, Alice, good morning. I'm a bit overexcited about what I've just seen on the news.' He paused in silent overture to his revelation.

'Something about Clive?' I prompted. 'Was Clive's death reported on the local television news?'

'Got it in one. They had no film footage, of course. The only media at the run was the local paper's photographer. But they've announced that it's now an official murder investigation.'

In a way I was glad there was no film footage, even though it would have been useful evidence. I wasn't sure I'd want to watch Clive running alongside all the other Father Christmases with his death only an hour away. Other runners catching the news would probably have a surge of survivor's guilt, not knowing at this stage whether the murder was targeted or random. After all, the apparent clue of the netsuke bear could be a complete red herring. Perhaps Clive's attacker had just been someone who hated Christmas and had picked a random Santa as victim. Now there could be Santas all over the Cotswolds thinking, *There but for the grace of God go I.*

'The television presenters did a dramatic reveal: "Father Christmas Fun Run Finishes in Fear", or some such alliterative headline,' Robert continued. 'Not much of a fun run for poor Clive. I expect now that the police have formally identified Clive, they'll be actively speaking more openly in hope of flushing out witnesses. It's not just you, Danny and Jack they've been grilling. When I went to fetch my copy of *The Times* from the village shop just now, Suki Price told me the police are working their way through all the runners registered, as well as the village folk who organised the race.'

'How did Suki know that?' I couldn't help but feel aggrieved that Suki knew more than we did, when Robert and I were the self-appointed sleuths.

'Oh, you know what Suki's like,' he replied. 'She's a gossip magnet, and as effective a broadcaster as the BBC, at least within the limits of her shop's catchment area. You do know, don't you, that if there's any news you want to get around the village, you only have to tell Suki in confidence? It'll be all over the village within twenty-four hours.'

I frowned. 'So, my *Parish News* magazine has competition?'

I could tell from the smile in his voice that Robert was amused by my defensiveness. 'Not at all. When people read the *Little Pride Parish News*, they know the content is reliable. Suki's method is always at risk of Chinese Whispers distorting the message in the process. That's one reason why Suki's gossip is always such fun – it's a heady blend of fact and fiction, and not to be taken seriously without a fact check.'

'So, did they say anything else about Clive? Presumably the police have secured a photo from somewhere to jog the memories of witnesses.'

'Yes, and what's more, they shared a few personal facts about him that might interest you, or at least, they did me.'

'Go on.'

'He was forty-seven years old, lived near Highbere, and worked at the city museum. Where they just happen to be running a Japonisme exhibition...'

'There has to be a connection! I can't believe Clive would have come down here for the Santa Run just by chance. Robert, I think we should go to visit the museum to see if we can find any clues there. Are you up for that?'

'Absolutely,' said Robert. 'But what am I thinking? Why did I phone you when it would have been almost as quick to walk around to your cottage? This is far too important a conversation to be having over the phone.'

'You're right,' I said, glad to be moving things along so quickly. 'I'll be opening the shop in a minute and firing up the coffee machine. If you're not doing anything else this morning, you're welcome to come round for as long as you like.'

'I'm on school pick-up for Tilly at three o'clock, but I'm free as a festive robin until then,' he replied. 'I'll be right there.'

'And as committed as a Christmas turkey after that,' I said with a smile.

I'd barely had time to put my phone back in my handbag when Robert was striding up the patio to my shop door, the most welcome customer that I could wish for.

30

HIGHTAIL TO HIGHBERE

I set a coffee in front of Robert on my shop's trade counter, and he sat in the 'care with the chair' seat that I'd rustled up for Maudie Frampton a few days before.

'What about abandoning the shop again? Aren't you terribly busy with the Christmas rush? There aren't many shopping days left until Christmas.'

'Mum will be happy to mind it for a few hours. She always is.'

'You'll miss her when she goes home to Norfolk after Christmas.'

I stared into the distance, picturing Mum's car driving off down the road.

'Yes, I shall,' I replied. 'The place will feel empty without her even if Danny moves back here afterwards. Things seem to be going very well for him and Jack, so I'm mentally bracing myself for Danny to decide to move in with Jack permanently.'

I produced the brochure from my handbag, spread it out on the counter before him, and tapped the picture of the netsuke bear.

'Goodness,' said Robert. 'I recognise that bear. Or at least, I think I've seen his twin.'

'I suppose it could just be a coincidence,' I demurred. 'And to be honest, I really don't mind if it turns out the police are right about the bear being a red herring unrelated to the murder. I'm not just doing this for fun, you know.' That wasn't entirely true. I was very much enjoying being thrown together with Robert as we joined forces to investigate. 'The most important thing is that justice is served.'

Robert smiled. 'OK, as long as you promise not to step beyond the bounds of innocent tourist behaviour. Besides, what's not to love about a pleasant day out together playing Cotswold tourists?'

I grinned. 'Great. I'll just fill Mum in on our plans. She's in the kitchen, reading a book and knitting, and she can do that just as well behind the shop counter, and with more daylight from the shop's big front windows. It'll be jollier too – we've far more Christmas decorations in the shop than in the cottage. I've barely had time to put any up in our living room.'

'While you do that, I'll bring my car around. Sorry the weather's not right for driving with the top down, but it'll still be a pleasant drive. I love seeing the architecture of the bare trees without their leaves. It's good to make the most of this before spring covers them all up again.'

Mum, to my relief, was entirely happy about the arrangement, especially when I told her she could bring her knitting. She had no other plans for the day. It wasn't as if she had local friends to meet for coffee or whatever.

'It's lovely to be needed again, dear,' she said as she settled onto a high stool behind the counter.

'And wanted, Mum.' I bent to kiss her cheek. 'And very much wanted.'

31

MUSEUM SECURITY

We found a parking space easily enough in the Chipping, the Cotswold word for 'market', where two rows of cars filled the spaces that on Wednesdays and Saturdays would be occupied by stallholders selling local farm produce and crafts. We parked in the shadow of an enormous Christmas tree, lavishly decorated with gold and silver lights and giant baubles in red, white and blue. Either side of the Chipping stood crooked rows of tall shops leaning against each other like so many drunken men doing their best to stay upright. The colour of digestive biscuits, they were built of local limestone. The shops had casement windows of tiny diamond-shaped leaded lights. From their size, these must originally have been built as the homes of wealthy merchants at the height of the medieval wool trade.

At one end of the Chipping towered a vast church with huge windows that must have filled the space with light – so different from the older, smaller churches at the heart of most Cotswold villages, including Little Pride.

At the other end stood Highbere Museum, a Victorian conversion of one of the larger merchants' houses. The museum had been founded by a local industrialist to coincide with the Great Exhibition in 1851, which had been designed by Prince Albert to celebrate all things British, at home and across Queen Victoria's Empire. Highbere Museum celebrated the local heritage from the Bronze Age through Roman invasion to the Industrial Revolution and beyond. This rich heritage, plus a generous endowment on the death of its founder, Sir Lewis Silver, the sugar magnate behind the Silver Sprinkle brand, had provided a future-proof legacy for Highbere, despite its founder's use of slaves in his Caribbean plantations.

'Coffee first?' asked Robert as he locked the car. 'Or lunch afterwards? Or both, I don't mind, as long as I'm home in time for Tilly.'

I glanced up and down the Chipping, appraising it for cafés.

'How about coffee in the museum café after our tour?' I suggested. 'Museum cafés are always worth a visit.'

'Sounds good to me.'

Robert took my hand and we strolled down the street, stopping now and again to gaze in shop windows.

It wasn't just Highbere's museum that was more upmarket than Broadwick's. All the shops were too, and their Christmas decorations. Elegant boutiques displayed beautiful clothes in the colours of the countryside. The lack of price labels told me these were clothes I couldn't afford. Specialist butchers hung game from ceiling hooks, presumably shot on local private estates. Artisanal bakers displayed loaves that looked as if they'd been shaped by sculptors, in every imaginable shade except the bleached white of supermarket sliced. A greengrocery festooned with holly and mistletoe was piled high with glossy tangerines and crisp Christmas dinner vegetables, along with exotic produce I didn't recognise. So, this was where to buy the ingredients I couldn't pronounce in recipes published in upmarket glossy magazines. This was aspirational Cotswolds indeed.

I stopped in my tracks outside a shop that looked oddly familiar. The window display was full of antique crockery and glassware, arranged to suggest a Christmas dinner was about to be served to an array of china-faced Victorian dolls and three huge threadbare teddies. The teddies reminded me of aristocratic Sebastian Flyte's beloved bear in Evelyn Waugh's *Brideshead Revisited*. I guessed present-day equivalents of the fabulously wealthy Flyte family were Highbere traders' ideal customers.

Beyond the shop window lay a beautifully curated mix of vintage furniture, fabrics and housewares. On the walls were bevelled mirrors of the kind that once hung above domestic fireplaces nationwide and original oil paintings and watercolours of bucolic scenes.

'It looks like your Curiosity Shop on steroids,' Robert remarked. I made a mental note of appealing ornamental touches that I might emulate in my shop – those that I could afford, anyway.

'Not for the likes of Little Pride, though,' I retorted. 'Look, that teddy bear costs nearly £2,000. I don't know whether that's the going rate for vintage Steiff, but it'd never fetch that much in my Curiosity Shop.'

Robert squeezed my hand. 'But your shop looks far more welcoming. There's only one customer in this one.'

I followed his gaze to the counter at the back of the shop, where I recognised a familiar figure: the hunched shoulders, dowdy appearance and unkempt hair of the vicar's wife, Mrs Shepherd. She was carrying a filled supermarket bag-for-life – the only one we were likely to see all day in this town where Provençal woven shopping baskets were de rigueur. Even at this distance, and with our view darkened by the ancient glass in the leaded windows, I recognised some of the vases lined up on the counter as the ones we'd seen Mrs Shepherd sorting in the vicarage, when she returned Robert's gift to him.

'She said she was taking all that stuff to charity shops in Highbere and Broadwick to avoid things being recognised by the people who'd given them to her,' I observed. 'But it looks to me as if she's trying to sell everything.'

Robert shrugged. 'That's up to her. They're her possessions, or rather hers and her husband's. Vicars don't earn much, you know, so I can understand her wanting to monetise unwanted gifts. Maybe she needs the money to pay for her Christmas shopping. What she's doing is hardly a crime.'

'I'm not judging her,' I said hastily, although conscious that I very much was. 'I'm just wondering why she felt the need to lie to us.'

'It's probably only the truly valuable stuff she's selling,' said Robert. 'No point in taking a lesser class of jumble to a shop like this.'

'I suppose not.'

I tugged at his hand to move him along, nervous lest Mrs Shepherd turn around and see us staring at her. It was none of my business really – unless she'd found the carved bear in the muddy fields when walking her dog the day after the Santa Run, and was now trying to sell this too. She seemed pretty discerning in her tastes. She might have recognised it as being worth cleaning up and selling.

'Free entry,' I noted as we pushed the revolving door into the museum lobby. 'There's a sign of a tourist attraction with no money worries.'

Just inside the lobby stood a large glass cube with a slot in the top for donations. Inside it was a foot-deep pile of banknotes and coins – a mosaic of copper, silver, blue and brown, peppered with other colours of higher denomination notes that seldom came my way. Next to the charity box was a card machine to accept electronic donations. I guessed their usual class of visitors didn't bother with loose change.

A smartly uniformed young woman with the smile and stature of airline cabin crew welcomed me with a warm smile at odds with her red-ringed eyes. She must have just heard of Clive's death and was nobly getting on with her job. For the first time it struck me that a good director would have closed the place for the day as a mark of respect for their late employee, and to give his former colleagues a day of compassionate leave to grieve. It's not as if such a thriving museum would miss a day's takings. Besides, with free entry, it was only the shop and café takings and donations that they'd miss out on.

When I told her this was our first visit, she produced from beneath the counter a laminated map showing the room layout on three floors. She tapped the largest room on the second floor.

'This is our special show just now,' she said. 'It's all about the influence of Japanese art on Westerners. It's one of the most interesting we've ever done. It's only temporary, so if I were you, I'd make sure you include it in your visit today, in case it's gone by the time you come again.'

We didn't need persuading.

We climbed the dog-legged stone stairs, admiring the paintings of prize bulls and country estates that hung in the stairwell, before reaching a broad carpeted landing. A large sign in the same font as the brochure directed us to the Japonisme display. Low lighting and soft, slow oriental music made me relax at once, and we progressed at a leisurely pace around the room, stopping to admire every glass case and read every information panel. The explanations were printed in a large, clear font, something I'd given up arguing the case for at Broadwick, which habitually used ten-point text to reduce signage costs.

We sat on a red velvet bench in an alcove to watch a film explaining the context of the exhibition and juxtaposing famous paintings by Westerners against the Japanese art that had influenced them. I'll never look at Klimt's *The Kiss* again without thinking of Japanese kimonos, or hear songs from Gilbert and Sullivan's *The Mikado* without remembering the artistic context.

'They didn't say much about netsuke,' I observed when the film concluded. Robert, in no hurry to get up from this cosy spot, put his arm around me.

'Maybe they didn't consider them as influential as paintings or textiles, or value them so much as status symbols. It seems people only collected them as ornaments, to put in display cabinets, rather than to wear, as they were originally intended.'

I was heartened that Robert had taken in what the film had told us, and didn't just watch it to humour me. I'm no cultural snob, but it boded well for our relationship if he took more interest in art and culture than, say, football and cricket, which leave me cold.

'But they said they have four netsuke on display here,' I said. 'So, it can't be just the bear pictured in the brochure. Let's go and find them.'

In almost the last case in the exhibition, we found what we'd been looking for: a glass cube dedicated to the art of netsuke.

The first we saw was a small white sheep, carved from some kind of bone.

'Imagine trying to carve a sheep!' I exclaimed. 'It can't be the easiest animal, with all that curly wool, but the carver has captured it well.'

Robert moved around to the next side of the cube. 'This coiled snake is pretty good too. Not only are the scales clearly marked, but the carver has even added a flickering forked tongue. It must be a tough wood for such a tiny appendage to stand up to daily use without losing its tongue, so to speak.'

Never keen on snakes, I overtook him to view the third side of the cabinet.

'My goodness, a carving within a carving!' I gasped. 'A song-bird within a cage. How can that even be possible? No wonder it could take months for the carver to produce a single object.' I had garnered that much from the video.

The fourth side of the cube was disappointingly empty, containing only a tiny empty plinth and a label.

'Ebony bear with emerald eyes,' I read aloud. 'Eighteenth century. Loaned by Norio Nagasaki. So where is it?'

Footsteps approached us from the far side of the gallery. I looked round to see a man of about thirty with auburn curly hair tied into a man bun. Inspired by characters in the Japanese woodblock prints, perhaps, although his baggy vintage tweed trousers, chequered braces and analogue watch marked him out as more of a hipster.

'Just in the nick of time!' he greeted us as he slipped a tiny key into the door of the empty side of the cabinet. 'Here you go. The missing link! I don't know where he's been hiding all this time. I haven't seen him since the second day of the exhibition.'

'Perhaps he went into hibernation,' I joked.

He held out his open palm, on which lay a small dark wooden bear with emerald eyes. I half expected the tiny creature to give us a knowing wink.

'I'm glad he's back so we can see him now, though,' I enthused. 'He's gorgeous. May I take a close-up photograph before you put him back in his cage? I love sketching carvings, and it's so much easier to get the details right without the glass of a display case blurring the resolution.'

I startled myself with this glib untruth. I may be artistic as far as needlework and knitting go, but I couldn't draw a bear to save myself from being savaged by one.

When the hipster assistant acquiesced, I pulled out my phone and zoomed in for a detailed photo before he could change his mind.

'I expect he just needed an emergency repair and had to be sent away to a specialist,' he said. 'Either that, or the guy who loaned him for the exhibition changed his mind and wanted him back for a bit. All I know is the boss just handed him to me with instructions to return him to his rightful case. Still, mine is not to reason why.'

I opened my mouth to speak when Robert butted in.

'Thank you very much,' he said to our new hipster friend. 'But we'd better dash now, Alice, if we're to grab that coffee before our parking ticket runs out.'

When he widened his eyes in warning at me, I nodded my head eagerly, like one of those carved red lucky cats so often on the counters of Chinese restaurants.

'Yes, of course, we must.'

As we sped away, leaving the young man locking the cabinet door, I whispered to Robert, 'Thank you for saving me from myself. Now let's go and have that coffee. I'm definitely feeling the need.'

32

CAFÉ SURPRISE

Robert kindly indulged my desire to sample the museum café. Such places usually cater to a high standard at reasonable prices, so are my go-to resort, if available, when I'm out and about and in need of a cuppa. As we queued at the counter to order, I explained to Robert my additional reason for staking out this one: to vet it on Danny's behalf, should he think of applying to work here.

You can imagine my surprise when after paying at the till we turned away from the counter and spotted Danny himself pouring a cup of tea from a fancy pot at the nearest table.

'Danny!' I cried. 'What are you doing here?'

'I could ask you the same question,' he replied affably. 'Come and join me, and I'll tell you.'

Robert set the cups from our tray onto Danny's table before going to return the tray at the trolley.

Danny took advantage of Robert's absence to tease me. 'Don't let me play gooseberry.'

'It's not a date, as such, it's a collaboration,' I replied in a whisper. 'We've come to check out the Japanese exhibition, in case it helped us to learn more about netsuke, to give us ideas about possible motives for the theft of the little bear.'

'And did it?' Danny was looking so pleased with himself as he sipped his tea that I wondered whether he was on the same mission and was one jump ahead of us.

'Yes, like you wouldn't believe!' I returned. 'While we were in the special exhibition gallery, one of the attendants returned to its case what looked to me to be exactly the same bear as the one from Mum's green scarf. How can we be sure it's not one and the same bear?'

Danny considered for a moment. 'Ask the owner? I mean, the person who's loaned it for the exhibition. I'm assuming it'll be on loan, rather than the museum's property, as it's a special exhibition. It's the sort of artefact that whoever possessed it would be very familiar with. They'd know every mark, every curve, every blemish – if indeed it had any blemishes at the time of the loan. If it's the one wrenched from Clive's scarf in a scuffle, it might have sustained new damage. I'm afraid I haven't had time to look at the display yet myself. I've had my mind on other things.' He lowered his voice. 'Actually, I've just had an interview. I didn't tell you before, so as not to jinx it.'

'Oh, thanks, so I'm a Jonah of job prospects now, am I?'

He grinned. 'No, sorry, that didn't quite come out right. I meant, I didn't want to tell anyone in case I didn't get offered the job. I actually applied on spec to this place some time ago, after the last round of redundancies at Broadwick. I'm as surprised as you are for me to be here for an interview now. I'd almost forgotten about it. Anyway, it's a terrific job, with more money, a better job title and free food and drink in the museum café during my working hours. If I'm offered the job, it would be hard to turn it down.'

'What does Jack think about it?'

'He's supportive. Highbere is not much further to drive from home than Broadwick, so it shouldn't really affect us. Me and him, I mean.'

When he said 'home', I wondered whether he meant my place or Jack's.

'Well done, Danny,' said Robert. 'This is a really smart museum, and it seems to be thriving. I imagine there are a lot of applicants for your job. How did the interview go, if you don't mind me asking?'

Danny held up his hands, splaying his fingers. 'No problem, Robert, I'm not superstitious. Actually, it was pretty good. It went by in a flash, which indicates a comfortable rapport with my interviewer. Adam Eden, his name is, and he's CEO.'

Laughing, I set my cup down on the table. 'What were his parents thinking? I hope they didn't name his sister Eve.'

Danny grinned. 'Don't worry, his name doesn't seem to have held him back. He's a sparky guy with some impressive plans and great ambitions for this place. I'd love to be a part of them, not just because it would look good on my CV. I'm genuinely excited about the prospect of coming to work here every day. I don't think I've ever felt that way at Broadwick. There are too many obstacles there, and too little investment. But Highbere, under Adam Eden, is set to become a model museum leading its field. I don't know how he does it, even with the recent grant they won from the lottery. He must be a whizz with money, as well as everything else.'

'That sounds wonderful. I'm almost inclined to apply for a job here myself.'

Robert gaped at me in alarm.

I reached across to lay a reassuring hand on his. 'I won't, though. Don't worry, Danny. I'll not be any competition. I'm too used to being my own boss now to work for anyone else again, and I love my shop, and Little Pride too. Honestly, I'm delighted for you. You deserve it. Go for it!'

Danny gazed down into his now empty teacup. 'Well, I'm not counting my chickens, not unless and until they offer me the job. You see, although most of the interviews seemed to go really well, it ended abruptly on a strange note. Which made me think it's not a done deal yet.'

'How do you mean?' I asked.

'We'd done the usual stuff of going through why I wanted the job and what qualified me to work here, and I felt as if I was giving all the right answers. Then just at the end, when we were talking about formalities such as potential starting date and what my travel plans were for the commute, he turned a bit cold. I've no idea why. I hate to say it, but I'm worried he might have suddenly twigged that I'm gay, and that he's a homophobe. Which I would never have guessed, as he seemed really open-minded and forward-thinking in every other respect.'

I gave Danny's hand a comforting squeeze. Robert leaned forward.

'There you go, Danny,' he said in a low voice. 'If it gets back to Mr Eden that you've been seen holding hands with a beautiful woman in the museum café, perhaps he'll offer you the job after all.'

'Which woman is that?' I sat back and gazed around the room.

Danny and Robert looked at each other, then fell about laughing.

'You, you chump,' said Robert, when he'd recovered.

Danny gave a sheepish grin. 'But seriously, Robert, if he is homophobic, I wouldn't want to work for him. That's just how it is.'

'I understand,' said Robert gently.

'By the way, Alice,' added Danny, 'I put your address down as my home rather than Jack's. I hope that's OK. Things are going really well between Jack and me, but I don't want to frighten him off by seeming to presume that I'm living with him for good. All the correspondence about the job so far has been online, but they needed my physical address today for Human Resources. I guess they have to make sure I'm not living on the streets or in a day release prison.'

'That's fine by me, Danny. I'm keeping everything crossed for you.'

33

ROBERT TO THE RESCUE

Danny left after he'd finished his tea, and we stayed a little longer drinking our coffee. Danny was planning to spend an hour or so strolling about Highbere to get to know the town a little better. After all, if he was to be offered the job, it would be useful to have staked out the local shops, restaurants, pubs and other facilities before he started working there.

I glanced at my watch as we left the café.

'I suppose we'd better head back to Little Pride so you're back in time for school pick-up,' I said. 'But before we go, can you please give me a few more minutes here? I'd like to pop back up to the Japanese gallery and photograph the bear's display label showing the lender's name. Then when I get back to my shop, I'll see if I can track him or her down online and send them Jack's photo of our bear, to see if they think it's actually his loaned bear on an unofficial outing from the museum. I'm not sure yet how that could possibly be, but as the attendant was just returning it to the display case after an unexplained absence, it's got to be a possibility.'

'Fine,' said Robert. 'I'll just sit here and read the exhibition catalogue while I'm waiting, to see whether that gives us any more clues. Come and find me when you're done.'

There was a display copy of the catalogue on a coffee table by the cutlery, along with high-end daily newspapers.

Back in the gallery, I soon found the name of the lender. 'Norio Nagasaki' meant nothing to me, but if he was a local, he should be relatively easy to trace. For all its apparent wealth, Highbere Museum would be more likely to source relevant exhibits as close to hand as possible to keep costs down. There couldn't be more than one person with a distinctive name like that in the Cotswolds, and maybe not even in the country.

Ten minutes later, Robert and I were marching sharply back to his car. While we'd been in the museum, the morning's drizzle had turned into a steady, heavy rain. As we approached his car, we noticed a little further along the marketplace a familiar grey Ford Escort estate with its bonnet up, and the back half of a lady in a dowdy tweed skirt and flat shoes, her top half delving into the engine. Robert dropped my hand to approach her.

'Mrs Shepherd, is that you?'

I don't know which he recognised first – the car or the rear end of the vicar's wife – but when Mrs Shepherd stood up, both Robert and I did a double take. Although she was wearing the same worn-out clothes as when we'd seen her through the antique-shop window, in other respects she had been transformed.

Her silvery hair was now a glossy chestnut with golden high-lights. Her unruly brows had been tamed into neat arcs. Her usually pale complexion was glowing pink all over, as if she'd just enjoyed a facial massage.

'Oh, my goodness, Robert, Alice!' Whether she was more flustered at whatever had gone wrong with her car or at our spotting her in Highbere, I was unsure. 'I've done something really stupid.'

'No, not at all,' said the ever-gallant Robert. 'You look wonderful.'

She clapped slightly oily hands to her face, dotting her pink glow with smuts.

'I didn't mean my make-over, but thank you. What I mean is, I've run out of petrol. I thought I had enough to get here, and I planned to call in at the petrol station to top up on my way home, after I completed my, uh, errands. But I've been over-optimistic. There's not enough to start the engine.' She ran a grimy hand over her professionally blow-dried hair.

'If that's your biggest problem, you're doing OK,' said Robert. 'And it's a problem that's easy to fix.'

Mrs Shepherd grimaced. 'But my husband and I aren't members of a recovery service. I suppose I'll have to push it all the way to the petrol station now.'

I bit my lip, and Robert coughed to suppress a laugh. 'Nonsense. My car's right here. I'll drive to the petrol station on the outskirts of town to buy an empty fuel canister, fill it up and bring it back to you. In the meantime, why don't you and Alice go and shelter from this awful weather in that cosy-looking café over there? It will be much more comfortable than waiting in a cold car.'

Mrs Shepherd gestured towards her tatty bag-for-life on the passenger seat of her car. 'Don't worry, I always take a flask of coffee when I go out anywhere very far. It saves so much money. It's probably lukewarm by now, but you're very welcome to share it.'

I slipped my arm through hers. 'Come on, I want to get out of this rain.'

She put up no further defence.

Inside Ye Olde Tea Garden, we sat amidst a surreal artificial landscape filled with fake greenery and flowers. I wasn't sure how to start the conversation. As I'd never been to a church service since moving to Little Pride, I was only on nodding acquaintance with the vicar and his wife.

Fortunately, a china pot of Lady Grey for two and a plate of lavender shortbread biscuits helped break the ice. Almost as soon as the waitress in Victorian dress had set our order in front of us, Mrs Sheppard covered her face with her hands and began to unburden herself to me.

'I was right, though, wasn't I?' She patted her restyled hair, now glistening with tiny raindrops. 'All that money I've spent at the hairdresser's is wasted now because I've been caught in the rain. Serves me right for being so vain. Talk about gilding the lily.'

I poured her a cup of tea, and mechanically she added milk.

'It's not wasted at all,' I replied. 'You look lovely. That hairstyle and colour really brighten your face, and a drop of rain won't spoil it. You look radiant.'

'That's probably a combination of the cold wind and the facial.' Her voice was grim. 'I hope to goodness the flushing wears off by the time Crispin sees me.' She stroked her sleek eyebrows with her fingertips. 'Though I don't suppose these will grow back by teatime. Not that Crispin will notice. He only ever says I look beautiful, even when I'm on my hands and knees in a scruffy housecoat scrubbing the kitchen floor. I think that means he never really looks at me properly. But just for one day, I wanted to look beautiful for my own sake. For this day. You see, today's my fiftieth birthday.' She scrunched up her eyes in horror. 'My fiftieth!'

She reached into her skirt pocket, distorted by the same-sized hard lump that I'd spotted in it at the vicarage. I took a sharp intake of break as she pulled the mysterious object out, then I sighed in disappointment. It was only a plastic dispenser of saccharine tablets. She clicked the top to drop two tiny white dots into her cup.

I stirred my tea.

'Take it from me as one who knows: fifty is the new thirty,' I declared. 'You'll look beautiful for more than just your birthday, in any case. You'll only need your colour touched up every couple of months to keep it up, and if you're worried about the cost of maintaining your eyebrows, just invest in a decent pair of tweezers. We all deserve a bit of regular self-care.'

I was speaking from the heart. I'd only realised after Steven had left me that I'd got out of the habit of my own self-care routine – something I'd revived only recently. Not just by getting Coralie to restyle my hair the week I moved to Little Pride, but also indulging in my love of knitting and other crafts, and making time to spend with my neglected, widowed mum.

'I know it's a cliché, but like the flight attendants say on aeroplanes: you must put your own oxygen mask on before you try to help others.'

Mrs Shepherd steeled herself with a long hard sniff, before dabbing her eyes with a linen serviette. 'I suppose you're right. It's not as if I've been using church funds to indulge my vanity, or even Crispin's stipend to treat myself. To pay for the treatments I've just had, I sold an old coral necklace I'd inherited from my aunt. I couldn't in all conscience wear coral, knowing what we know now about the damage being done to coral reefs, but in Aunt Madge's day, no one dreamed a coral necklace was a bad thing. So, I thought I might as well sell it, and then use the money for something I really did want. That, and the odd few pounds I've made from selling the fruits of my

Swedish death cleaning. Most of the clutter I've cleared out has been fit only for charity shops, and I suspect some of it will have been put straight in the bin the moment my back was turned.' She sat up a little straighter, seeming to rally slightly. 'But I think I deserve the little I have been able to make, as recompense for all the trouble I've gone to clearing out my house, don't you?'

Although I positively enjoyed decluttering and housework, I could tell Mrs Shepherd was at the opposite end of the tidiness spectrum. Having a huge, old-fashioned vicarage to look after rather than a cute, compact cottage like mine probably didn't help. I wondered how she'd spent her time before she had married the vicar, and how different her life might have been now if they'd never met.

'Did you spend all the money, or have you any change?' I asked, an idea forming in my head.

'I have about £25 left over.' She sniffed. 'I was thinking of blowing some of it on a bunch of flowers on my way home. Crispin always tells me to buy myself a treat on my birthday, and I usually buy something practical like tights or underwear, but I was in the mood to be a little more frivolous for a change.'

'I've got an even better idea,' I declared. 'Let me show you.'

As soon as we'd finished our tea and shortbread, I led her to a charity shop a few doors down, whose window display shouted to me that inside lay a very high class of jumble, donated by the good burghers of Highbere.

When we returned to her car, which by now Robert had refuelled from the petrol can, Mrs Shepherd, or Grace, as she insisted I now call her, was clutching a carrier bag filled with a gorgeous olive-green shift dress, gold-tone earrings and a cashmere forest-green cardigan, bagged for just £25.

'I can't thank you enough for your encouragement,' she said

to me as we hugged our goodbyes. 'Do you know, I think I might even go back to that clothes shop again.'

Oblivious to the continuing drizzle, Robert and I watched her drive away before we returned to his car.

'I may not be a churchgoer,' I said to Robert as I fastened my seatbelt, 'but I think today I may have scored a point with Him upstairs.'

34

THE CARING CHAIR

With plenty of time to reach Little Pride before the end of the village school's day, Robert suggested stopping halfway home for a quick lunch at an old Cotswold coaching inn, The Golden Fleece. Over warming bowls of homemade leek and potato soup and sourdough rolls, we reviewed our eventful morning.

'Fancy bumping into Danny!' I began. 'And what about Grace Shepherd? What a dark horse, slinking around Highbere like that selling the family silver!'

'Be fair, Alice, she had told us she was decluttering, and it's not as if the vicar wouldn't have known what she was up to, with the stuff spread all over the living room like that. She probably just didn't feel comfortable telling us that she planned to sell some of it, fearing it might make the vicar look uncharitable.'

'Oh, I'm not judging her for it. Actually, I'm glad I helped persuade her to spend more of the proceeds on herself. How sad that the vicar's finances are so desperate that selling an heirloom is the only way she can afford a new hairdo, even though it was an heirloom she didn't want in the house for reasons of conscience.'

I slathered some ivory-pale, unsalted butter onto my sourdough roll, regretting the need to disfigure the pretty rose-shaped butter pat.

'We are right to assume it was her only her own stuff she was selling, aren't we?' said Robert. 'I mean, just because she's married to a man of the cloth doesn't make her incapable of breaking the law for her own gain.'

'If so, she's a fine actress. She seemed really upset when I took her into Ye Olde Tea Garden. A combination of embarrassment, self-admonition and misplaced humility.'

'But the netsuke,' Robert persisted. 'Could she have tried selling the netsuke bear to an antique dealer after stealing it, only for the dealer to recognise it from the exhibition brochure and threaten to report her to the police if she didn't return it to the museum straight away?'

'Here's another idea. She might have somehow stolen the bear from the museum, then held it to ransom. The owner wouldn't have been exactly thrilled to know the museum had effectively lost his little treasure that was meant to be in their care. Grace Shepherd might have realised that, and threatened to tell Norio Nagasaki unless the museum's management paid her to return it to them. She could easily have visited the museum before we bumped into her, to hand over the bear in return for the ransom money. Maybe the ransom money was what paid for her haircut, and who knows what else she might have spent it on.
'

He had a point. All that fuss about decluttering and her birthday could have been to put us off the scent.

'Anyway, I vote we chase up Mr Nagasaki to see if he knew his little bear had gone missing from the museum, and to see whether he thinks the bear on Mum's scarf was his bear, or whether it's a worthless fake.'

'It's a pretty crucial link in our theory,' said Robert. 'It still seems odd that we saw Grace Shepherd in a distressed state just after we'd seen the real bear returned to its plinth after being absent from the exhibition all weekend.'

By now I was hoping she was innocent. 'She might have found the bear by chance in the rec, guessed it came from the Japonisme exhibition, and returned it for no payment at all, like the good citizen that you might expect a vicar's wife to be. She'd know that exhibition was on, as she's been a frequent, if secret, visitor to Highbere lately.'

Robert dropped me off outside my shop before driving up the high street to collect Tilly from school. I thought Mum would be glad to see me back when I entered the shop, but she didn't seem to be missing me at all. She was perfectly happy sitting and chatting to Mrs Jorkins. Both were knitting at high speed, Mum on her little green Lloyd Loom chair, and Mrs Jorkins on my 'care with a chair' seat. Two cups and saucers and a large teapot were on the counter, beside a plate bearing a few telltale chocolate biscuit crumbs.

'Oh, hello, dear.' Mum laid down her knitting for a moment as I lifted the flap to pass through the counter. 'There's still some tea left in the pot if you fancy joining us? Just fetch yourself a cup.'

'No thanks, Mum, I've just had coffee after my lunch.' My lips twitched in amusement. 'But don't let me interrupt you.'

She sat back down and resumed knitting.

'We've been having such a lovely chat,' said Mrs Jorkins. 'Your mother kindly said I'm welcome to stop as long as I like, so I did. In fact, I went back to get my knitting. Still, I suppose I'd better be getting back to Mr Jorkins to start getting his tea ready.'

'Come again soon,' Mum told her with a cheery wave. 'And do bring that pattern book you were telling me about.'

I planned to wait until the shop door closed behind Mrs Jorkins before saying any more about this unexpected knitter-in-residence, but Mum spoke before I could get a word out.

'It's so lovely to be making new friends down here,' she said. 'Gladys Jorkins is such a nice lady.' Gladys? How come Mum knew Mrs Jorkins's first name before I did? 'Maudie Frampton has been telling everyone about your special caring chair, and Gladys is the fourth person to take advantage of it today.'

'Take advantage' is the right phrase to use, I thought, but what I said was, 'I don't suppose she actually bought anything? Not even the cup of tea?'

Mum looked away. 'Well, if I was in my own house having a friend in for a cuppa, I wouldn't charge her, would I? Nor did Mrs Hardy ever charge me.'

It seemed odd to me now that neither of us used Mrs Hardy's first name. But then I remembered that Mum did when she was talking to her directly. The formality was for my benefit, maintaining the same formal distance as if she were my schoolteacher.

A realisation hit me with the force of a falling piano landing on my head: how lonely Mum must have been since first Dad's death, then Mrs Hardy's. How could I be so mean as to begrudge her inviting a new Little Pride friend in for a friendly knit and natter? If I'd found them chatting like this over tea in my kitchen, charging her guest would never have occurred to me. Swiftly I backtracked.

'That's fine, Mum, you can have Mrs Jorkins round' – I almost said 'to play', subconsciously parenting the parent again – 'whenever you like. She's a dear old soul. And any other new friends you make here. Treat my house as your own.'

As I spoke, I realised I meant every word.

Perhaps it was proving easier here in Little Pride for Mum to make new friends than in her home town, where many people wouldn't recognise their neighbour if they bumped into them in the street.

'Anyway, if you're happy out here in the shop for a bit longer, I just need to look something up on my laptop that's better done in the privacy of the kitchen rather than at the shop counter.'

'Oh dear, you're not ill, are you? Consulting Dr Google?'

I had no idea where she'd picked that up from. She didn't even own a computer at home. Danny, maybe? Or Jack?

'No, Mum, don't worry, I'm fine, thanks. I'll tell you later, if I'm successful.'

Happy enough with that, Mum took her tape measure out of her knitting bag to check whether she'd reached the casting-off point on her cardigan sleeve.

35

LOCATION, LOCATION

I'd expected Norio Nagasaki to have a Japanese accent. Instead, the voice on the other end of the Zoom call was that of a languid Californian.

'It's a piece from my grandfather's netsuke collection,' he told me, before taking a long puff of a slender cigar.

I waited for him to exhale, the cloud of smoke a visual drum-roll to his announcement of how expansive that collection might be.

'It's modest compared to the number owned by some of those rich Europeans at the height of the Western craze for Japanese art,' he continued. 'I have just a half dozen pieces, but all very fine. That I have any at all is a testament to the friend-ships my grandfather had built with his Californian neigh-bours before his family was interned during the Second World War.'

Of course, the war. A long-buried memory of a school history lesson flashed into my head. The USA, I recalled, sent all its Japanese residents to alien holding camps for the duration of hostilities, no matter how long or how peaceably they had lived and worked in America. They lost their homes and all their property in the process.

'My grandfather entrusted one piece of netsuke to each of his American friends, rather than giving his whole collection to a single person for safekeeping. All seven promised to restore them to him on his release.'

I looked down at the notes I was scribbling as he spoke. 'Hang on, I thought you just said you had a collection of six. Or do you mean the seventh is the one you've loaned to Highbere Museum?'

He closed his eyes as he took another deep draught from his cigar. Just when I was beginning to think he'd absorbed all its smoke, he tilted his chin upwards to blow a series of small neat smoke rings, then watched them rise like netsuke-sized halos above his head. *The sign of an active volcano* were the words that popped into my head from nowhere.

'One of his American friends let him down. So now I have six pieces, including the bear in Highbere Museum.'

'I'm sorry,' I said, feeling strangely responsible for the Caucasian's betrayal. 'But I'm glad the other six true friends delivered. It's very kind of you to lend even one of your pieces to the museum under the circumstances.'

I wondered what had brought him to Oxfordshire. Presumably he was now resident, or at least staying long enough to loan personal possessions to a local museum exhibition.

I wondered how much to reveal to him. I didn't want to cast aspersions against the museum by suggesting it had been remiss in its safeguarding of his precious possession. So I had planned an alternative strategy, and I chose my words carefully.

'It's about your netsuke bear that I'm calling. I gather it's very valuable, a rare piece by one of the best eighteenth-century netsuke-shi.' I hoped that by using the Japanese name for a carver of netsuke, Norio Nagasaki might think I knew more than I did.

'The bear is unique,' said Norio, matter-of-fact.

'Then please don't take my question the wrong way – or rather my observation. But I run a small shop in the Cotswolds, and it seems that an identical piece to your bear passed through my shop recently.'

His voice lost its Californian sunshine. 'I'm afraid I'm not in the market for expanding my collection,' he said, tight-lipped, as he turned his cigar around to consider the glowing tip. 'For one, I don't wish to pay today's collectors' prices. For two, the only pieces I desire are my grandfather's. They are a part of my grandfather and the heritage he bestowed on me. That is why they are priceless to me.'

'Please don't worry,' I tried to reassure him. 'I'm not pitching to sell you anything. I just wanted to show you a photograph of the one from my shop to see if you think it's a good match for yours, or at least made by the same craftsman.'

'OK, try me, baby,' he drawled. 'But I can tell you now, yours'll be a phony.'

I clicked *share screen* on the Zoom menu, then expanded Jack's photograph of the bear on the scarf to full screen, while keeping open a thumbnail window at the top right of the monitor so that I could still see Nagasaki. I saw him drop his cigar on his lap with a whispered curse. He retrieved the cigar, set it in a groove in an onyx ashtray on his desk, and brushed what I assumed to be fallen ash from his leg.

'Tell me this, Ms Carroll. What's your game, sewing my grandfather's precious bear to some weird homespun cloth? The green doesn't even match his emerald eyes. It's pretty crass.'

Emeralds? No wonder this little creature was in demand,

whether or not he was fashioned by an ancient Japanese craftsman.

'Please don't think I'm doubting your authority, but what makes you so sure it's your bear?'

Norio tapped his screen with one hand, forgetting I couldn't see which part of the image he was pointing at. 'See that little ringlet beneath the bear's right eye?'

'Yes, or at least I do now that you've pointed it out.'

'No bear has naturally curly fur. That spiral was the secret signature of its maker. My grandfather's grandfather was this little fellow's netsuke-shi, and my other five are his work too. He made all seven for a particular customer who supplied the jewels for the details, but he died before he could settle his bill. So my ancestor kept them. I guess he was wary about selling them on to someone else, after the commissioner died. I'm told he was a superstitious fellow, but perhaps it was a welcome excuse to retain some of his works of art for himself.

'I don't know how much you know about the craft of netsuke,' he continued. 'But many netsuke-shi did not overtly sign their pieces, not so much from modesty, but because they felt the pieces belonged to their commissioners. If anyone should be boasting about them, it should be their eventual owners. But this curl was how my ancestor made sure he could always recognise one of his pieces if he saw it again. And so, when my grandfather crossed to the USA in 1932, he took them with him, hoping they'd bring him luck. Did they hell. He had to start from scratch financially in 1945.'

I kept scribbling as he spoke. He kindly paused to let me catch up with him, waiting until I looked up from my notebook before continuing.

'OK, now it's your turn to spill the beans, Ms Carroll. What is my bear doing in your shop and stitched onto some crazy crafting thing? How did the guys at Highbere deem it appropriate? Their insurance only covers it while it's in their care on their property. They have no business letting it off their premises, let alone allowing it to be mounted on a piece of knitting. That's an insult to the craft of the silk weaver and kimono maker whose precious fabrics the netsuke would have once adorned. I'll have something to say to Adam Eden about his negligence next time he buys me lunch.' Eden was buying lunch for his supporter? Was the museum really that rich? Surely it should have been the other way around? 'When I last saw it in the museum display case, at the private preview of the Japonisme exhibition, it was perched on a gleaming Perspex plinth above a mirror to reflect the underside, and that's where I expected it to stay.'

When he paused for another puff of his cigar, I took the opportunity to reassure him.

'Please don't worry, Mr Nagasaki, that's exactly where it is now. I've been at the museum today and admired it just as you described.'

He shifted in his seat as he stubbed out the cigar, a thin column of white smoke spiralling up from the slab of onyx into the air.

'Then why the weird picture here? Or is that some fancy Photoshop trick? Are you pitching for the rights to reproduce my bear as an accessory for some knitwear line? No can do, Ms Carroll. I'd never licence the cheapening of my ancestor's craftsmanship. Putting it on some hillbilly handknit is blatant cultural appropriation.'

I held up my hands in surrender. 'No, no, that's not at all my intention. I'm simply looking into a puzzling occurrence. I'm afraid I can't tell you the ins and outs of it just yet, because I haven't got to the bottom of it myself. When I do, I'll be sure to let you know. But the important thing is, your netsuke bear is safe as houses in Highbere Museum. In the meantime, thank you very much for your time, Mr Nagasaki. You've been more helpful than you can imagine.'

I hastened to close the conversation and end the call, lest I inadvertently give away more than I wanted him to know – including the fact that the bear at the heart of Clive's murder had disappeared for weeks from Highbere Museum – and then, just as mysteriously, been returned.

36

BUTTONOLOGY

'The person who stole the bear from Clive must have known it belonged in Highbere Museum, or else how could they return it so quickly?'

Robert filled our glasses while he considered my question. 'Perhaps that was why Clive had stolen it from Wendy's stall. As a Highbere employee, he knew its provenance and was keen to restore it.' He set the bottle down again on my kitchen table. 'But why would someone steal it from the museum, and put it in your shop, and then take it back again?'

'It seems more likely to me that the average thief would steal it to sell it on the black market,' I said. 'Not just play musical chairs with it.'

'Ah, but I think they did sell it,' returned Robert. 'To you. It seems you unwittingly bought it from someone as part of a batch of second hand buttons.'

'But we know I didn't.' I tried not to sound hurt, but I was a little offended. 'Haven't we shown its photo to all the people who I bought buttons from, and to Nell Littlewood too? None of them recognised it. Nell knows I didn't too. She even suggested someone else had put it in my shop without me knowing, rather than selling it to me.'

'Yes, but none of the women we're talking about are exactly young. Can we really be sure that they'd remember what every single button in their possession looked like?'

'Are you saying you don't trust their memories? That's a bit rich, considering Grace Shepherd is a decade younger than you.'

'Although, to be fair, I suppose it is pretty memorable, as buttons go,' he demurred. 'Wendy certainly thought it remarkable, because she picked it out for special treatment.'

I put my head in my hands. 'Well, I believe Maudie Frampton and Mrs Jorkins and Grace Shepherd, even if you don't. But the only other option is that the bear somehow liberated itself from its museum display case, prowled all the way down here, broke into my Curiosity Shop and stowed away in one of my button boxes when I wasn't looking.'

Laughing, Robert sat back in his chair and raised his glass to admire its contents against the overhead light. The wine glowed golden yellow.

'Highbere to Little Pride is an awfully long way to prowl,' he said. 'Maybe it hitchhiked. Like those cats you hear about on the news every now and again that turn up hundreds of miles from home, after climbing into a car or lorry and going to sleep.'

I grinned. 'Perhaps our bear had an accomplice?'

I lifted my glass, hoping the cool, fresh drink might calm my racing mind. But before I could take another sip, I slammed my glass on the table, splashing a tidal wave over its rim.

'An accomplice!' I cried. I wasn't smiling now. 'An accomplice who planted the bear in my shop to incriminate me in its theft.'

'But it didn't work, did it? Because nobody has accused you of stealing it. In fact, we have no evidence the museum even knew it was missing, apart from that guy who was returning it to its display case when we were there this morning.'

I slapped my palm on the table again, this time making the half-empty bottle jump. Robert grabbed the bottle, as if fearing that in my excitement I might overturn the whole table.

'You're right,' I replied. 'But someone else knew it was in my possession,' I continued. 'Think back now to the ransacking of Coralie's tiny house. Did I tell you about that peculiar customer who came in asking to see my buttons the day after Martin's visit? He claimed he was a button collector.'

'Are there such things as button collectors?' He sounded dubious.

I got up, marched over to my desk and pulled out from one of the cubbyholes a slim paperback to show him: *Buttons* by Alan and Gillian Meredith.

'But this guy was creepy. He just didn't seem like a normal button collector.'

Robert smirked. 'How could you tell? Were all his clothes fastened with Velcro and zips?'

That made me chuckle. 'It's no joke, though, Robert. He made me feel really uncomfortable. Besides, I've never had anyone else in my shop asking for buttons. It's a curiosity shop, not a haberdashery. Then he was going on about looking for a particular type of button that sounded to me like a toggle. Which is why I told him I'd given all my toggles to Coralie for her jewellery making.'

'So, you sent him round to see Coralie?'

'No, that was the last thing I wanted to do. I just gave him her Etsy shop URL. But he could easily have extrapolated her address from that if he'd bought something from her online, and then seen the return address label she'd stuck on the package. I happen to know she uses her real home address rather than a box number for her dispatches. So, hey presto, Mr Button-Collector knows exactly where to look next. Not that he could find the bear, no matter how he hard he looked, because it simply wasn't there. It was under my counter all along, among the fancier buttons that I'd hidden from him. And there the little bear stayed, until Mum ferreted him out when seeking special buttons to finish off her Christmas knits.'

'Only later, at the fair, for Clive to liberate the bear, complete with scarf,' Robert concluded. 'That makes perfect sense. Alice, is there any chance that your button collector and Clive could have been one and the same person? You know how it is, sometimes, when you see a familiar person out of their usual context, and you can't place them in that different setting. Might Clive also have ransacked Coralie's tiny house looking for the bear there, only to give up and find it later on the scarf at the fair?'

I covered my eyes with my hands.

Robert pulled his phone out of his pocket and tapped in a search string. He held up the television news story to show me. Unfortunately, the report did not include a photo of Clive, just a long shot of a couple of hundred of Santa-alikes at the starting line of the fun run. Clive could have been any of the runners – except the female ones, that is. (Now that would have been an even better disguise.)

It was time for some lateral thinking.

'How about the museum website?' I suggested. 'Museum websites quite often have photos of staff doing stuff, or a list of team members with photos, or blog posts with staff bylines and headshots.'

Robert tapped away at his phone screen for a moment.

'There's a Meet the Team tab in the menu on the home screen,' he announced. To my surprise, rather than click on it, he turned his phone face down on the table. 'Listen, Alice, we must be careful here. If I just show you the photo of Clive, it'll be too easy for you to say, "Yes that's him, that's the button collector," because it's what you want to believe. What the police would do is to give you lots of people to choose from, not just show you the prime suspect.'

Mum, who had been reading Mrs Jorkins's pattern book in the sitting room, wandered into the kitchen.

'You mean like an identity parade, dear?' she said mildly, dropping a camomile teabag into her favourite mug. She'd been with me long enough now to have decided which was her favourite mug.

'Yes, that's exactly what we need, Mum!' I startled her by shouting in my excitement. 'Robert, can you mock up a pretend identity parade for me, scraping pictures of random men off the internet, as well as Clive? That's if they haven't taken his photo off the museum website yet.'

Robert picked up his phone to look at the search results again, but held it close to his chest so that I couldn't see the screen. He scrolled down the page then gave a wry grin.

'At last, a bit of good luck,' he said. 'Guess what Clive's job title was? IT manager. Presumably in a team of one, because his mugshot is very much still on Highbere's website.'

37

IDENTITY PARADE

We decided to head next door to his house, so that Robert could disappear into his study for a little while to scrape a selection of photos from the internet and print them out. It seemed a better idea than looking at smaller portraits on his phone screen. I waited for him in his kitchen. Soon he was spreading a neat line of a dozen prints along the breakfast bar.

'Don't they usually have only five or six suspects in a police identity parade?' I queried. 'At least in cop programmes on the telly, anyway. Not that more isn't a good idea. The police probably keep the numbers down because it's easier than rounding up more volunteers, not to mention cheaper, if they actually pay the people. Anyway, a false positive seems a lot less likely with a wider choice.'

Taking a deep breath, I marched to the far end of the breakfast bar to begin my examination, feeling like a general inspecting his troops. At each photo, I stood still for a moment, giving the candidate my full attention. At the first four, I shook my head and sidestepped to the next one. But the fifth made me gasp.

'It's the button collector! I'm sure this one's the button collector! I recognise his distinctive square jawline.'

A chill ran through me, as I saw him in quite another guise: pallid and cold on a mortuary slab.

Robert remained admirably dispassionate. 'Keep going, Alice. You're not done yet.'

Obediently, I moved a step to my left to view number six, then seven. Nothing. Then at number eight I gasped aloud.

'Martin!' I squealed. 'That's Danny's Martin.'

I turned to face Robert, hands on my hips. 'This is hardly a random selection off the web. I'm not supposed to know anybody here.'

I seized the photo and turned it face down, not wanting to look for a moment longer at the man who had caused both Danny and me so much trouble in the past.

'Keep going,' was Robert's only reaction.

I tried to put Martin out of my mind and focus on the task in hand.

'I recognise number nine as well, but I can't think where I've seen him before. And ten looks vaguely familiar, but I don't know why. This is getting weird.'

'So do I,' said Robert, to my surprise. 'Cast your mind back to our outing to the Japonisme exhibition at Highbere. I swear he was the young man restoring the bear netsuke to the museum case.'

A ring at Robert's doorbell made us both jump, as if we'd been caught in the act of some devious crime.

'I'll go,' said Robert, marching out of the room.

'Well, it is your house,' I murmured after he'd left the kitchen. 'Or had you forgotten?'

I smiled at a fleeting fantasy of my being chatelaine of his beautiful home. My cottage next door felt like a doll's house in comparison, albeit one kept by very houseproud dolls. Housework is one of my superpowers.

'Danny! This is a nice surprise!' I said, as my friend entered the room. I immediately regretted my words, hoping Robert didn't take them as an indicator that I wasn't enjoying our evening *à deux*.

'Sorry to call in out of the blue, but when I knocked on your door just now, Alice, Wendy told me you were here at Robert's,' said Danny, as Robert filled a tumbler with sparkling water. Danny is teetotal. 'I hope you don't mind me inviting myself in, Robert, but I need a bit of sympathy, and I didn't want to offload onto Jack.' He took a sip of his drink.

'It's the Highbere Museum job,' he said, leaning back against the counter and closing his eyes.

My heart skipped a beat. 'And?'

'I didn't get it.'

Just as well, I thought, given that I'd just discovered Martin was working there. But now was not the time to drag up the wretched Martin again. What Danny needed was sympathy.

I dashed over to give him a bear hug.

'I'm so sorry, Danny, especially when you thought the interview had gone so well.'

'Most of it anyway, until towards the end. So, it's back to the drawing board for me.'

I released him from my embrace. 'If they're not smart enough to hire you, it's their loss. They don't deserve you. You'd be an asset to any decent museum.'

Robert patted Danny's shoulder in commiseration.

'Take heart, Danny,' he added. 'I'm sure there'll be another job out there somewhere waiting for you, and it'll have your name on it.'

Danny forced a smile. 'Kind of you to say so, Robert, but I

must admit my confidence has taken a bashing. I don't know what I could have done better at the interview. Perhaps they wanted a local person who could walk to work. It was only when I said where I lived that Mr Eden turned a bit cold. Maybe it had taken him that long to work out that I was gay, and he's a homophobe. Oh well, it can't be helped. I'll have to put it behind me and move on. Maybe I'll wait until after Christmas before I apply for any more new jobs, to put some distance between this disappointment and any fresh opportunities.'

'Yes, relax and enjoy Christmas,' I urged him. 'Now, come and sit down here and tell me what you and Jack are planning to do over the holidays. Lucky Jack to have a fortnight off from school!'

'I wish Broadwick City Museum closed for the school holidays,' said Danny. 'But as you know from experience, Alice, it will be heaving with kids all over the Christmas break.'

Taking another sip of his drink, he wandered over to join me, pulling out one of the high stools to sit at the breakfast bar.

'Hello, what's this?' he asked, tapping Clive's photo. 'This is the murdered Santa, isn't it?'

I punched the air in victory. 'Yes! I thought it was, but if you think so too, it must be him. You saw him for much longer than I did when he was lying on the ground.'

Robert laid a finger on number ten. 'Do you know, I think I recognise this one from the Santa Run also. He got the booby prize as last to cross the line, but he didn't seem very pleased about it. When the photographer asked him to pose with me for a photo, he stomped off, scowling.'

'Where was his Christmas spirit?' I retorted.

Danny's face was stern.

'Actually, I know who that one is too,' he said slowly. 'That mole above his upper lip makes me absolutely certain. I was having trouble keeping my eyes off it at the start of the interview.'

'Interview?' I echoed. 'What were you doing interviewing the speeding Santas? Was Jack making a promotional video ready for next year's Santa Run? I know teachers are organised, but that's exceptionally far-sighted of him.'

'Oh no,' said Danny. 'I wasn't interviewing him. He was interviewing me at Highbere Museum. Meet Adam Eden, Highbere's high-flying chief executive.'

38

MUSEUM PIECES

I turned to Robert accusingly. 'Robert, where exactly did you lift these photos from? It's an extraordinary coincidence that not one but three of them should be recognisable from Highbere Museum.'

Robert looked away. 'OK, I confess, I may have been a little bit lazy and just raided the Highbere Museum website. They've got loads of headshots on their Meet the Team page. I thought there might be such a thing as a type of person who works at a museum, and that I'd end up with an assortment of similar chaps. If you could pick out Clive from this line-up of museum staff, your identification would be more dependable than if chosen from a broader section of society.'

I raised my eyebrows at him as I pointed to Danny and myself. 'Exhibit A: both Danny and I worked at Broadwick City Museum, and nobody would get the two of us mixed up.'

'Nor would you confuse either of us with Adam Eden,' added Danny, tapping the dandyish headshot of Highbere's CEO.

'Sorry, I didn't really think that through,' said Robert. 'Even so, my strategy worked. Alice reliably identified Clive, Highbere's

IT manager, as the button collector. Singling out Highbere's CEO may also be relevant, as he was also at the Santa Run.'

'I'll raise your button collector a strangled Santa,' said Danny. 'Before Alice joined us on the rec, Jack lifted Clive's fake beard to check it wasn't hampering his laboured breathing. We both got a good look at his face then. But then we put back the beard as we thought it might help keep him warm and dry. It was raining quite hard by that point in the afternoon.'

'That's pretty conclusive,' said Robert. 'But what are we to make of all this? It doesn't get us any closer to Clive's murderer.'

'At least we now know his boss, Adam Eden, was also at the Santa Run, probably not intending or expecting to make himself conspicuous by coming last in the race,' I said. 'That explains why he was so ungracious about winning the booby prize. He didn't want the attention.'

'He'd have been less conspicuous if he'd worn all the gear but not bothered running,' Danny observed. 'And if he was in on the theft of the netsuke with Clive, why did they both need to be there? The bear was only a couple of inches long, and the scarf lightweight.'

'It's not as if they were stealing a bulky or heavy thing requiring two strong men to lift it,' I pointed out. 'I know Mr Eden didn't look at the peak of physical fitness, but I reckon he could lift a scarf and a button on his own.'

'A scarf and a netsuke,' Danny corrected me.

'Do you remember seeing the two of them together at any time during the run or the fair?' I enquired. 'It's possible they weren't operating together. They might not even have known the other was there.'

'I don't remember seeing either of them talking to each other or to anyone else,' Danny said. 'Nor did I spot Adam Eden in the village hall. A Santa of his girth would be hard to miss. Not many of the runners had stomachs that completely filled their baggy red coats, making the buttons gape.'

'Maybe Adam Eden had commissioned Clive to buy the scarf in order to return the netsuke to its rightful place at the museum, but he didn't trust him to keep it safe,' Robert suggested. 'Perhaps he thought he might sneak off and sell it on the black market and run off with the takings.'

'Can a netsuke be so valuable that someone would risk their career and their reputation to do that?' I asked.

'Everyone has their price,' said Robert. 'Whether the little bear matched Clive's price is the next question. Let's search online for the highest price ever paid for a netsuke.'

He pulled out his phone and tapped in a suitable search string, quickly finding some useful figures.

'The art auction house Bonhams' record for a single piece of netsuke is half a million US dollars. That was exceptional, but five-figure prices seem not uncommon – decent sum if you consider dollars per gram, but not enough to keep you for the rest of your life – especially if that life must be lived on the run.'

'It's a bit sad if Adam Eden didn't trust his own staff,' I said.

'Maybe Clive had financial issues that made him vulnerable to temptation where money was involved,' suggested Robert. 'Maybe credit card debt, or bailiffs threatening to repossess his house, or even someone blackmailing him, poor fellow.'

I was impressed that Robert, who presumably hadn't had money worries for decades, was the first of us to think this.

'Do you think that's why Clive stole the scarf instead of paying for it?' said Danny. 'He couldn't even rustle up a fiver?'

'That seems unlikely,' I replied. 'He wanted to get in and out of the fair quickly and as surreptitiously as possible. I'm guessing this was his first such crime as he was so bad at it.'

I looked at Danny for a reply, but something had distracted

him. He was staring into the distance with his mouth open. Then he leaned back on his stool, his face pale.

'I was wrong about Adam Eden,' he said. 'You know I said how well the interview was going until we'd nearly reached the end, and he suddenly turned cold, which made me think he might be homophobic?'

As we nodded, Danny ran his fingers through his tight dark curls.

'But now you realise he wasn't homophobic, but racist?' Robert surmised.

'I don't think so. You see, I've just remembered what we were talking about when his tone changed. He was asking me about how I'd commute to work if I got the job – whether I had a car or would rely on public transport. I said no, I'd need my car, because there's no public transport serving Little Pride. When he realised I came from Little Pride, it must have dawned on him that I might have seen him and Clive at the fair. As far as I know, the media never revealed that Jack and I were the people who found Clive after he had been attacked. But Adam Eden must have reckoned there could be a chance I'd seen them behaving suspiciously. Apart from all the Santas, most of the villagers always turn out for the fair. That means as a resident of Little Pride, it was pretty likely I would have been there too. Whatever he was up to, whether in cahoots with Clive or acting alone, he didn't want to risk hiring me, in case I was on to him. He couldn't get rid of me fast enough.'

'There you are, I told you it wasn't your fault you didn't get the job,' I reminded him.

He sat up a little straighter, apparently reassured.

'So what exactly were the Highbere duo to up to?' asked Robert. 'And how will we find out?'

'If we were in the middle of Broadwick or Highbere, I'd say

check the CCTV footage,' I replied. 'But out here, the only CCTV is on people's doorbell cameras and home security systems.'

'I don't suppose anyone was videoing the race?' Robert said hopefully.

Danny shook his head. 'The local paper sent their photographer to take stills, and I guess he would have sought permission from anyone he snapped, and I expect some of the runners and their supporters will have been filming or taking photographs on their phones. But Jack told me some entrants ticked the "no filming or photography" box on their Santa Run application forms. That stopped the organisers filming any of it, because it would be too much hassle to edit out the runners with specific race numbers.'

'Race numbers!' That sparked a new idea. 'Can you find out which numbers Clive and Adam wore? And whether they registered in their real names? If there are no Clive Thatchers or Adam Edens on the entries database, we'll know they were trying to hide their true identity. Then we'd be right to be suspicious of their motives for taking part.'

'I don't know,' said Danny. 'But I know a man who does. Give me a minute, and I'll get Jack to check the database. The master is stored on the school computer system, but I know he has a print-out of it at his flat. I've seen it on his desk.'

He left the room to call Jack in private.

'We're getting closer,' said Robert, slipping his arm around me.

I smiled at him. 'Closer to each other or to the murderer?'

'Both,' he said, planting a gentle kiss on my hair.

39

MINING THE DATA

'No and no.' Danny was beaming as he returned to the sitting room. 'Neither Clive nor Adam registered under their real names. Neither are on Jack's list. I can't remember what Adam's race number was, but I know Clive's was 112. I spent long enough on Saturday staring at it, watching his chest rise and fall to monitor his breathing.'

'If Adam wore 111 or 113, that would suggest they were working together, because if they'd booked at the same time, they'd have been assigned consecutive race numbers,' I said.

'I thought at the time it was an odd coincidence that Clive should be 112, the phone number a lot of other foreign countries use for the emergency services instead of our 999,' said Danny.

'And I can tell you Adam Eden's race number,' said Robert. 'As you know, as the "real" Santa, I got race bib number one, even though I wasn't running. But I was presenting the prizes, and I had to shake hands with the winners in all the different categories. I don't mean to sound unkind, but when I presented him with the booby prize as last person to cross the finish line, I remember looking at his number as I presented his award and thinking the number III was appropriate, because he'd make three of me.' He flushed slightly, as if embarrassed at this confession of being judgemental.

'I'm sorry, that makes me sound rather vain,' he apologised.

I patted his thigh affectionately.

'Just as well you were, because that's a really helpful piece of evidence,' I said. 'So it seems likely now that Adam registered at the same time as Clive, so they may well have been working together. I wonder whether Adam came into the village hall after the run, like Clive did? But if they came to steal the scarf, why did it take two of them? We could really do with more information about their characters, but where can we get that, when they seemed to be taking pains to avoid contact with other people?'

'Ask Suki,' said Robert. 'Suki might be able to fill us in on Clive at least, because she wouldn't have let him enter the village hall without buying raffle tickets. He might also stand out in her memory because she wouldn't have recognised him from the village.'

'But weren't there a lot of outsiders running?' I asked.

'Yes, but many of them have been taking part in our Santa Run for years, some of them to the point that they're almost honorary villagers,' said Robert.

'OK, then, let's try Suki,' I said. 'It can't do any harm. Even if she doesn't recognise him, at least we'll know we've tried.'

I checked my watch. 'Suki's Stores will be closed by now, so shall I phone her at home?'

Robert grimaced. 'I wouldn't if I were you. She's very protective of her privacy out of hours.'

'I don't blame her when she spends twelve hours a day on public view in her shop,' said Danny. 'Jack's a bit like that with his teaching job. That's why he doesn't choose to live in Little Pride, even though it means he has to commute by car rather than walk to work. He doesn't want to be bumping into kids and their parents and carers during his own time, like doctors whose friends consult them at parties about their bad backs or worse.'

Robert folded his arms. 'I can relate to that. I don't get people asking my advice about their washing-up, but they do tend to bug me about other things once they know who I am, especially trying to tap me for donations to their pet projects. I like to choose the charitable causes I donate to, not to be hustled into supporting other people's.'

'Back to the point,' I said. 'Let's tackle Suki tomorrow morning.'

'What a pity I'll be at work,' said Danny. 'I know she opens at the crack of dawn, but I can't face getting up early enough to drive here before doubling back to Broadwick.'

'Don't worry, Robert and I will speak to Suki first thing.'

'Shall I call for you at nine a.m., to catch her between the school run and your own shop's opening hours?' Robert offered.

That was in any case my most usual time to shop there, topping up my tea-room supplies before the start of my working day. I'm often the only customer in the shop then.

'Yes, please,' I said. 'Now let's work out our strategy for questioning her. Danny, you can role-play Suki.'

Danny spluttered. 'Actually, I think it's time I went back to Jack's flat. But let me know tomorrow how you get on, and I'll message you in the meantime if I remember anything else about Clive or Adam Eden or the fair that might be relevant to our enquiries.'

'By the way, Danny, before you go, let me tell you something else that we've discovered today that might make you glad you didn't get the Highbere job.'

'Go on,' said Danny.

'Martin works there now. That identity parade of photos that

Robert showed me earlier – they were all taken from the Team section of the Highbere Museum website. And one of them was Martin's headshot.'

Danny's jaw dropped, then after a moment, he gave a wry grin.

'Looks like I dodged a bullet there,' he said.

As he headed for the shop on his way home, I was pleased to see the spring had returned to his step.

40

QUESTION TIME

As it turned out, we didn't need the list of questions I'd prepared for Suki. Always ready to gossip, she started a monologue of complaints about Clive as soon as Robert showed her his photograph.

'Oh, him? Miserable git. You know, he was the only person all day long not to buy a single raffle ticket. I don't expect everyone to buy a strip of five. We're not all made of money, which is why we sell single tickets too, so that everyone can afford a flutter. But it's better than charging admission, because at least you have a chance of winning a prize. So, it's not the done thing to refuse to buy a raffle ticket. Not that he didn't try, mind you, or at least pretend to try. He offered me a credit card in payment for a strip of the things, and when I told him I couldn't accept it, he pulled a handful of other credit cards out of his wallet and told me to take my pick. Well of course, I didn't have a card reader, so I couldn't take any of them. Who buys raffle tickets by credit card anyway? In my shop, I never let my customers buy National Lottery tickets with anything but cash. That would be the thin end of a slippery slope, and I don't want it on my conscience that I've sold someone lottery tickets they can't afford. But that Clive fellow, he can't have been skint. I could tell from his watch.'

'Eh?' I was struggling to keep up with her. 'Oh, you mean he had a smart watch?'

'No, one of them posh gold ones. I almost didn't let him in on principle, but then I thought, someone as flash as that might be a good prospect for some of the stallholders. Some of the traders have card readers or take payment on their phones, but not all of them. You have to encourage people to buy as much as possible, or else the stallholders won't come back next year.'

'Very sound,' said Robert soothingly.

'So did you let him in?' I ventured.

'Yes, and do you know what? He only stayed about five minutes, and all he bought as far as I could see was a boring, cheap scarf. What a tightwad. Then I heard he hadn't even bought that because it turned out he nicked it.' Suki caught my eye and clocked my vicarious offence on Mum's behalf. 'Oh, sorry, Alice. I mean, he stole a very nice piece of knitwear off Wendy's stall.'

Since when had Suki been on first-name terms with Mum?

'Fancy upsetting your lovely mum like that.' Suki was redeeming herself now. 'Didn't do him no good, either, I gather.' That was an understatement. 'Not that I'd wish strangulation on anyone but he had it coming to him.'

Talk about harsh! But then Suki always did talk tough. I knew that underneath she had a kind heart.

'I've just been reading about him in today's paper,' she continued.

She nodded at the newspaper open on the counter in front of her and jabbed a fingernail at Clive's photograph on the front page – the same headshot that was on the museum website.

'Seems like the police haven't got much to go on yet,' she

added. 'They're just blaming some unknown gang after him for debts, like a poker ring or some such. That sounds a daft idea to me. If he was in debt, he should have pawned that fancy watch of his.'

Just then, Suki's mobile trilled, and she took it to the far end of the shop to answer it.

'Then the police might be glad to hear our new theory about Adam and Clive being somehow in league,' I said to Robert in a low voice. 'Do you reckon the police should be our next stop?'

I turned the newspaper around to face us so that we could more easily read the story.

'I suppose it can't hurt,' said Robert. 'In fact, one might argue we're duty-bound to help the police with their enquiries.'

'OK, let's just pop home first, and I'll ask Mum to mind the shop while we drive into Slate Green and visit the police station.'

'Again? Are you sure she won't mind?' asked Robert. 'If you prefer, we could leave it till this evening after close of business, or I can go in by myself. Not that I wouldn't rather be with you.'

A warm glow rushed through my body.

'I'm sure she won't mind,' I replied. 'She had a lovely time yesterday while we were out, with Mrs Jorkins bringing in her knitting and having tea with her.'

'OK, then. Let's brace ourselves to do our citizenly duty, and we'll be on our way.'

41

DOWN AT THE STATION

I defy anyone walking into a police station not to feel a little nervous, as if they're about to be rumbled for some inadvertent misdemeanour. I was no exception, clinging on to Robert's hand for comfort as we approached the desk. Although I was a little offended that the front desk officer addressed Robert rather than me, I was glad not to be there on my own.

'We'd like to speak to whoever is in charge of the investigation into the death of Clive Thatcher in Little Pride at the weekend,' said Robert. 'We have some information that may be of value.'

The officer wrote a note on the jotter in front of him. 'There's no financial reward, sir, if that's what you're driving at.'

Robert's voice turned terse. 'It's justice we're interested in, not money.'

The officer laid down his pen. 'As you like, sir. I'll just summon my colleague, sir.'

He stepped away into a back room, where he remained. A senior officer emerged from the doorway and strolled to greet us.

'Good afternoon, sir, madam,' he said. 'Detective Inspector Williams. How can I help you?'

After we'd introduced ourselves, he invited us to follow him down a corridor to the left of the counter. Robert and I marched in step with him as if we were on parade, having a little bit of fun to try to put ourselves at ease.

The detective inspector led us into a starkly decorated room. Actually, not so much decorated as doused with the bare minimum of steel-grey paint to cover the bricks in the walls. He beckoned us to sit down on plain, hard plastic chairs on one side of a Formica-topped table, while he took the comfier padded chair on the other side.

Then he produced an electronic tablet from the inside pocket of his tunic, tapped it a few times and paused to fix me with an enquiring stare. I felt as if he was assessing whose side I might be on, the victim's or the murderer's, before taking my name and contact details. Then he repeated the process with Robert. I half expected him to offer us the statutory single phone call allowed to the newly arrested, but all he did was sit back and clasp his hands on the table in front of him.

'So, what is this new evidence you would like to bring to our attention? Fire away and as much detail as you can remember.'

I leaned forward, pressing my forearms onto the chilly plastic surface of the table.

'The thing is, Detective Inspector,' I began. Was that the right way to address him? I wondered. I didn't want to offend him by getting his title wrong before we started. I took a deep breath before continuing. 'We have discovered that Clive Thatcher's employer, Adam Eden, was also present on the day of the unfortunate assault.' I couldn't quite bring myself to say 'murder', although that was what it amounted to – or perhaps manslaughter, if it was somehow accidental, and Eden meant only to intimidate Clive into surrendering what he had stolen.

Detective Inspector Williams tapped a few notes onto his tablet. Then he clasped his hands again and looked up. 'And that is significant because?'

Dry-mouthed, I swallowed before continuing, wishing I'd thought to bring my water bottle with me. 'We think Adam Eden may have commissioned Clive Thatcher to steal the scarf for the sake of the netsuke sewn onto it.'

The detective inspector looked up from his tablet, his fingers paused over the on-screen keyboard.

'Net what?' He frowned. 'Suki? She's the lady who runs your village shop, isn't she? Where does she come into this?'

Still wary of offending him, I suppressed a smile. I felt in a stronger position now. I spelled the word out for him letter by letter: 'N-E-T-S-U-K-E. It's a kind of antique Japanese button, and the one that was sewn onto the scarf that Clive stole was shaped like a bear. My mum knitted the scarf.'

In silence, Detective Inspector Williams reread what he'd just typed, his lips moving as he tried to make sense of his notes. 'So, you think that Clive Thatcher and Adam Eden were in league to steal a kiddie's button?'

'Oh, no, Detective Inspector, it wasn't for children. Netsuke were especially crafted for Japanese gentlemen in the Edo period.' I spelled 'Edo' out also to spare him the need to ask.

'Why exactly do you think they wanted to steal your mother's scarf?'

He was missing the point.

Robert tried to explain. 'They didn't need to steal it. She was selling her handknits on her stall at the Christmas fair for a fiver each. So, they could easily have bought it, but they didn't. Which makes the whole business more suspicious. Especially if the netsuke officially belonged to the museum, or at least was on loan from it. Why should they be so surreptitious about taking back what was technically theirs? We thought at first that Clive must be acting alone. He stole the scarf and made a dash for it out of the hall. Then, as you know, my friends Danny and Jack found him shortly afterwards, apparently having just been violently attacked with the scarf.'

Detective Inspector Williams unfolded his arms. 'Look here, madam, we knew all this already, from the evidence your friends and neighbours told us initially. All you have added is that the button on the scarf was made in Japan. That's hardly a novelty. Loads of stuff in our shops is made in Japan, Hong Kong, China, Taiwan. It certainly doesn't make something worth stealing.'

I leaned forward in my chair, making it rock onto its two front legs menacingly. 'What's new is that we now know Clive's boss from the museum where he worked was also taking part in the Santa Run, and that they registered together under false names.'

'Don't tell me. They signed up as Father Christmas and Saint Nicholas.'

I bit my lip. Why wasn't he taking us seriously? I crashed the back legs of my chair onto the ground, making him jump. 'The thing is, we have seen the very same netsuke at the museum, in a special Japonisme exhibition, featuring only genuine antiques. We think it's very valuable.' I didn't bother to explain Japonisme to him. If he wasn't going to make an effort to follow what I was saying properly, I wasn't going to help him more than I had to.

'So, what was a museum piece doing on your mother's scarf?' Now he seemed to be more on board.

'You may well ask.' I thumped the table with the flat of my hand for emphasis. 'But we think a further thief had been involved, and that Adam Eden knew about that. He then enlisted Clive Thatcher to recover the netsuke for the museum, before the owner who'd loaned it to the museum got wind of its disappear-ance. Its theft would have got Adam Eden and the whole museum into terrible trouble.'

'So, this Mr Eden instructed his IT manager to steal a scarf and run off with it – oh, sorry, with just the teddy bear sewn onto it – and then strangled him as his reward?' He pushed his tablet away slightly, as if he was done with recording our conversation. 'Then I'd say Mr Eden's management techniques could do with a little work.'

I couldn't argue with that, but he was rather missing the point.

'I'm sorry, love, but if this netsuke bear was so valuable that someone had nicked it from Highbere Museum and given it to your mum as some kind of fence' – I flinched at the very sugges-tion – 'why didn't this Mr Eden call the police, rather than sending some minion to pinch it back? The law was on his side, so what had he to fear?'

Firstly, I'm not your love, I wanted to say, *and secondly, who are you to refer to Clive as Adam Eden's minion?*

For the sake of trying to keep the detective inspector on side or even to get him on side, Robert said in a conciliatory tone, 'We haven't worked that out yet, but we do think there's a good chance Adam Eden was Clive's attacker.'

Whether or not Detective Inspector Williams realised he was shaking his head in disbelief, I'd already got the message that he was once again dismissing my theory out of hand.

When I slumped down slightly on my seat, he must have realised I was feeling deflated, because his tone softened a little.

'Listen, love, I know you're just trying to help, and I've made a note of your concern on our files.' The police officer hadn't given his tablet a single tap since his bad joke about management training. 'But we're already quite a long way down the line with our enquiries and, off the record, I can tell you that we believe it has nothing to do with Adam – your Mr Eden – or anyone else at the museum.' His left eye gave a barely perceptible twitch as he formalised the museum boss's name, but it didn't get past me. 'We've already spoken to Mr Eden in the course of our inquiries, in his role as Clive Thatcher's employer, and he told us that Clive was going through some personal problems related to his online gambling habit and consequent debt. We think that caused some kind of breakdown, and accounts for his erratic behaviour, unaccountable theft of the scarf, and impulsive self-harm.'

'Are you seriously suggesting he tried to strangle himself with the scarf?' asked Robert. 'That's absurd.'

'It's an unusual choice of suicide method, I grant you, but not all such events are textbook.'

Textbook? Since when was there a textbook about suicide methods? I squeezed my eyes tight shut as I remembered Clive's final words: *'Net... net...'*

'We suspect it may have been a cry for help, madam.'

Ah, so I'd been promoted from 'love' to 'madam' again, now that I was hearing him out.

'A cry for help that went tragically wrong,' the detective inspector continued. 'Between you and me, I expect this sad case to put a damper on the sales of scarves this winter.'

As if I had any intention of taking fashion advice from a police officer.

Then an alarming thought struck me. Supposing he accepted that the netsuke on the scarf had been stolen from Highbere Museum? Supposing Adam Eden had reported the bear had been stolen, and the detective inspector's apparent obtuseness was a cunning plan to make me confess to being in receipt of stolen goods? What was to stop him accusing Mum of its theft, or me?

At that point I became impatient to end our discussion and flee the police station as soon as possible.

I gave Robert a sideways look, willing him to get us out of there. He obliged.

'Well, thank you kindly for giving up so much of your valuable time, Detective Inspector. We appreciate the opportunity to share our thoughts with you, but we're relieved and reassured that you're completely on top of the case. We'll be on our way now and leave you to it.'

Detective Inspector Williams tapped his tablet again, presumably closing his file of notes, or possibly sending it straight to his trash folder. By this time, the latter would have been fine with by me.

Robert and I almost ran down the steps of the police station, before flinging wide his car doors, leaping inside and slamming them behind us.

'It's Adam Eden,' we said together.

'He's mates with the local constabulary, isn't he?' I asked, wide-eyed.

'Yes, and they're accepting the yarn he's spun them about Clive attempting suicide with the scarf to escape from online gambling debts,' said Robert. 'I don't believe that for a moment, do you?'

'Absolutely not. Now, our priority is to find Adam Eden and get him banged to rights.'

The corners of Robert's mouth twitched in amusement. 'I don't know, you spend half an hour with a police officer, and you come out speaking like a character in *The Sweeney*. But if you're right, I'll do everything I can to help you.'

'Does that include inviting Adam Eden out to lunch?' I said sweetly.

'What? Why?' In his surprise, he stalled at the traffic lights and had to restart the engine.

'Because I reckon that's the easiest way to extract the evidence that we need to incriminate him. At least, it's the easiest legal way.'

He steered us onto the lane that led to Little Pride. 'And the easiest illegal way?'

I licked my lips. 'It crossed my mind that I might go to visit to him posing as a plain-clothes detective and quiz him.'

'Yes, that would definitely be illegal,' he said. 'Now, fill me in on the details of your legal plan.'

In my excitement, I wriggled in my seat. 'You arrange to take him to lunch, posing as a potential wealthy donor.'

'But I am a potential wealthy donor,' he said cheerily. 'Although as I said before, I choose my beneficiaries with the utmost care.'

'Good. That's even more legal, then.'

'You can never be too legal,' he said, deadpan. 'Then what, Detective Inspector Carroll?'

'You discreetly quiz him about the museum's financial situation. I have a new theory, you see, stemming from my conversation with the nearest thing I've found to a wealthy Edo-period Japanese man, Norio Nagasaki. He was horrified at the idea that his precious bear had been allowed out of the museum, because the museum's insurance only covered it while it was under their roof. What if that was sufficiently alarming to Adam Eden that he'd go to any lengths to find and get back the missing bear, because otherwise he'd not only incur the wrath of a museum benefactor, but also risk his reputation, and the museum's, for not safeguarding items on loan? If word got out that he'd allowed the piece to be stolen, no other collector or museum would ever want to loan them anything again. It would drastically reduce

Highbere's appeal if it could only ever display what it actually owns.'

As I waited breathlessly for his reaction, Robert blinked a few times. 'But do you think that potential reputational damage would be enough to make him physically attack Clive, even if he didn't intend to kill him?'

'If his job is his life, it might do. And if Clive really did have gambling debts, Eden might not have trusted him not to sell it once he'd taken it back. The resulting scandal might be enough to close Highbere Museum down, and then he'd struggle to get another job in the world of museums too. He'd be regarded as a Jonah.'

'Are you thinking I can get some kind of confession from him just by taking him to lunch?'

'No, but he's more likely to reveal the truth about the museum's finances. Supposing he's been cutting corners to fund his ambitious plans – such as not insuring exhibits on loan? Besides, he's all the more likely to accept an invitation to lunch from Robert Praed, philanthropist, if the museum is in financial trouble.'

'You don't know how much of a philanthropist I am,' he teased. 'I keep that sort of information completely to myself. The same might be true of my money.'

'It doesn't matter,' I declared. 'I can pose as your PA and phone up to ask for a lunch appointment with you. Your known wealth will be too much of a temptation for any museum director to turn down, whether or not you've ever donated a penny to an organisation of that kind.'

'I suppose so,' he demurred, as we turned in to Little Pride high street. 'But I can save you the trouble of pretending, Alice. I can get my actual PA to phone Eden's office right away.'

He had a PA? Of course he did. Picturing a glamorous Miss

Moneypenny type, I batted away a twinge of jealousy. He seemed oblivious to my concern, adding, 'My PA in England, anyway. I have several dotted about the globe.'

He pressed the button to open the gates to his drive, and as the gravel scrunched beneath the tyres, I should have been beaming in anticipation of pinning down a ruthless murderer. But my spirits were dampened by the dawning realisation that despite Robert's frequent shows of affection to me, perhaps I was punching above my weight. I wondered whether he'd also delegate buying my Christmas present to one of his harem of PAs. But for now, I had to put that thought out of my mind. First, we had to catch up with Adam Eden and bring him to justice for the murder of Clive Thatcher, because now we knew one thing for certain: if we left that to the police, it wasn't going to happen.

42

APPETISER

'How did Clive know the stolen netsuke was in Little Pride?' asked Danny when I phoned him that evening to update him on progress.

'That's easy,' I said. 'You told me yourself how meticulous and knowledgeable Jack is when he's doing anything online.'

'Yes.' He sounded unsure where this was leading.

'Well, as we both know from briefing Broadwick's IT guy about items for their website, he'll have added loads of metadata to his posts about the Christmas fair. You know, the descriptions and keywords you're meant to add to image files, to explain them to visually impaired people who can't see them, and to make images easier to find in an online search.'

'Yes, but doing it for a business enterprise is quite different from sharing something just for fun. Jack's not an IT professional.'

'No, but he's very thorough. Ask Jack what metadata he added to the photos he used to promote the various bazaar stalls. I'm willing to bet you a month's rent he put in enough details to allow anyone to track the missing bear online.'

'Steady, Alice!'

I could contain myself no longer. 'Because, you see, when I put in a search string earlier, along the lines of "small dark brown wooden bear carving near me December 2025", what do you think it came up with?'

'No!'

'Yes! Jack's photo of Mum's scarf, complete with our little wooden friend. Clive Thatcher, as an IT boffin, would have found it as easily as I did, and probably faster. And when better to steal it than when it was on public display in the middle of a busy, noisy Christmas fair? Especially if disguised as just one Santa among a couple of hundred. So much easier than when it was still in Mum's knitting bag. His boss thought so too. Why else would a clearly unfit Adam Eden have enlisted in the Santa Run himself?'

'OK, let's assume Eden had directed Clive to retrieve the netsuke at the fair,' said Danny. 'Why did he need to come too?'

'Because he didn't trust him. Even so, he couldn't do it himself, because he didn't want to be seen to be involved in its recovery, to protect his reputation. Remember, none of us saw Eden at the fair. Suki verified that for me this afternoon, when I took Eden's photo to show her. She didn't remember him from her raffle stall, and you know no one gets past Suki selling raffle tickets without her giving them the third degree.'

'So, Eden trusted Clive to pick up the scarf, but not to bring it back to him?'

'Yes, and I know why,' I said. 'We've already discussed that the likely value of the bear could be substantial, but not enough to keep a thief on the run for life. However, I picked up some useful inside information when I went to visit the police station earlier. An officer told me that their line of enquiry is now connected with Clive being desperate to clear online gambling debts. An addicted gambler not only has a warped idea of how lucky they are – anyone who believes online gambling companies' promises of big winnings are deluded – but also, they'll do rash things to save themselves, regardless of what normal people would see as a huge risk.'

'So, even if Clive was untrustworthy and secretly planning to sell the stolen bear for his own gain, why didn't he just pay the fiver to buy it?'

'He literally didn't have any cash,' I surmised. 'An IT boffin like him probably only ever pays with his phone. Suki thought he was fobbing her off, being too mean to buy raffle tickets, but when he offered her credit cards to pay for them, and she had to turn him down because she didn't have a card reader, he was probably genuinely disappointed. As a gambling addict, he'd probably have been sure he'd had a chance to win, and his judgement was temporarily clouded by the excitement the prospect of winning brought. By the time he reached Mum's stall, he'd probably twigged that making an online transaction connecting him with the fair would have been a bad idea. It would have left a clear trail of evidence between himself and the netsuke – a rookie error he would avoid.'

'That makes sense,' said Danny. 'So, have I got this right? You think someone stole the bear from Highbere Museum. When Eden found out, he realised it would cause immense reputational damage to himself as CEO and to the museum as a whole. It could even be the end of his career and of the meteoric rise of the prestigious museum in his care. So, he briefed Clive to find the bear, which he did, thanks to Jack's well-tagged photo on the Facebook page for the Christmas fair. Then he commissioned Clive to fetch it from the fair, but he didn't trust Clive to hand it over to him, due to his own financial troubles. So, he let Clive do the dirty work of picking the bear up from the fair, then snatched it from him as soon as he came out of the village hall. Whether or not he intended to strangle Clive in the process, we cannot know. But we can assume that he headed back to Highbere alone and unnoticed, while we were still tending to poor Clive. When you and Robert visited the museum the following Monday, you saw the bear being returned to its display case, and the museum attendant we spoke to couldn't account for why it had been missing over the weekend.'

'No, he just said "the boss" had given it to him and told him to put it back – which I assume means Adam Eden.'

'Perhaps Eden wasn't meaning to murder Clive, but he just wanted to put Clive out of action during his getaway,' said Danny, always ready to see the best in people. 'Eden came last in the Santa Run, remember, so it's a fair bet that Clive would have caught up with him, even if his boss had a head start.'

'I'm thinking Eden may have bribed Clive into stealing it,' I continued. 'Because he knew about his gambling debts, and that he would welcome an unofficial bonus. Or he might have threatened to sack him from his job at the museum if he refused, leaving Clive in even worse financial straits.'

We fell silent as this sank in.

'There's just one thing that doesn't stack up,' said Danny at last. 'How come the little bear was in your shop when it should have been safe under glass in the museum? And if Clive was also the button collector who came to your shop supposedly in search of toggles, but actually expecting to find the netsuke bear there, how did he know it was in your shop? That was way before Jack had put the photo of the bear on the Christmas Fair's Facebook page. It was prior to your mum's return to Little Pride. For all I know, she might not even have knitted the green scarf at the time.'

I wrinkled my nose. 'That's two things. I'm going to need a little more thinking time.'

43

THE SAVVY EXECUTIVE

'Good news, Alice,' said Robert, striding into my shop late the following morning. 'I've managed to organise a lunch date with Adam Eden tomorrow. I expected to have to wait for a gap in his diary, but my resourceful PA, Teri, managed to persuade him to make it sooner by telling him I'd be leaving the country soon and was keen to see him before I left.'

My shoulders sagged. 'Oh. Where are you going?'

I hoped it wouldn't be for too long. I'd thought he was taking time off until the new year. Would it mean he'd be away for Christmas? Perhaps he was off to relax in some luxury sunny spot, such as the Maldives. I didn't blame him. Besides, Christmas on my own here with Mum would still be fun, with the village looking and feeling so festive. We'd even been thinking about going to the Christmas Eve Midnight Mass together for the first time in decades. All we needed now was a bit of snow, and Little Pride would look like a scene from a Christmas card.

'I'm not going anywhere,' said Robert.

Trying to mask my involuntary sigh of relief, I ended up coughing instead.

'That was just Teri's little deception to secure an early appointment. So, I'm meeting him for lunch at one o'clock tomorrow, at the Red Kimono in Highbere.'

'Splendid. Am I invited?' I hoped I might pass for one of his colleagues.

'Yes and no.' Robert made himself comfortable on my 'care with a chair' seat. 'That is, if you approve my proposal.'

I drew in a sharp breath in surprise, before realising he didn't mean that kind of proposal. 'Tell me more.'

I perched on my stool, resting my elbows on the counter and my chin on my hands.

'As we discussed before, I chose the sushi restaurant so that I can easily direct the conversation on to all things Japanese, including the exhibits in the museum's current exhibition. I'm also going to grill him about the museum's financial management and resources, in hope of getting him to confess that they're struggling. After all, he won't want me to think their finances are hunky-dory, for fear I might take my millions elsewhere to a needier cause. With my business hat on, I'm a crack negotiator, Alice. You've never seen that side of me.'

'You have a special business hat?' I teased him. 'Is it made of the same materials as your everlasting sponge? An everlasting hat would be an interesting sideline.'

He grinned. 'I'm talking about my metaphorical business hat, and you know it. What I mean is, I can be irresistibly assertive in conversation, persuading people to disclose information they hadn't intended to. I'm not saying I can wheedle a confession out of him, but I can certainly find out more information. I hope it will be enough to tell us whether or not our theory about his involvement in the theft is correct, and maybe even that he was Clive's assailant.'

'So where do I come in?' I was worried that as an incompetent liar, I might have trouble playing along with his charade.

'You are to enter the restaurant ten minutes or so after Eden and I arrive, and perch up at one of the counter-side seats. The restaurant has one of those rotating conveyor belts around a central counter, serving sushi between twelve and two. It's not uncommon to see people dining alone there, so you won't look conspicuous. Your task is to be on standby, in case I tip you the wink to call the police. If that happens, don't tackle Eden physically. Leave that to me. I am no black belt, but I'm confident I can corner him within the confines of our booth, and keep him there till the police arrive. I hope that may not be necessary, but if it is, your role will be invaluable.'

I thought this over for a moment. He may have been sixty years old, but he was lean and fit, with quick reactions. Eden was maybe fifteen years younger, but as we knew from the Santa Run, he was not on top form physically.

'OK,' I said at last. 'Just promise me one thing.'

'What's that?'

'You won't wear a scarf.'

44

YO! NETSUKE

The next day, Robert and I drove in his car to Highbere and found a parking space in a quiet side street, less conspicuous than in the Chipping, where we had parked before. We didn't want to risk being seen arriving together if Adam Eden happened to be strolling through the marketplace on his way to the Red Kimono, the most direct route from the museum. After a quick hug and a kiss for luck, Robert cut back through the chilly drizzle to the Chipping, and I headed in the opposite direction. I planned to walk around the block a couple of times before arriving at the restaurant.

Turning right and right again took me to the far side of the museum entrance, and I was relieved to see its CEO heading away from me towards the Chipping. I wasn't due at the restaurant for another ten minutes, so I decided to kill time by popping into the museum, where at least I could wait somewhere warm and dry.

I climbed the steps and entered the old-fashioned revolving door. As I was about to emerge into the museum lobby, I recognised another familiar back: Martin's. He was standing between me and the big Perspex collection box, choosing a key from a massive bunch to unlock the door. He must have been a key holder to just about everything in the museum. In his other hand, he held a grey bag of coarse weave, the sort made in prison workshops for post offices and banks. I guessed he was about to empty the collection box to bank the proceeds.

I kept walking, following the circular path of the revolving door. Fortunately, nobody else was approaching to enter or leave the museum. I figured if I went round a few times, that would give Martin time to finish his task and head back up the stairs to his office, before I entered the lobby.

On my second circuit, a familiar sound struck my ears: the tinkling of numerous tiny objects, as Martin plunged his hands and wrists into the mass of banknotes and coins. On the third time around, he was mixing them up for fun, letting the coins trickle through his fingers before transferring them into the bank bag. I recognised the twisting and turning of his hands, the way he had when he... when he what?

Taking baby steps to slow the door's revolutions, I tried to think where I'd seen him do that before. Not at Broadwick City Museum, where donations went into a slot in a wall-mounted box. There you had to remove a steel drawer to empty it.

No, it came back to me now. It was when he'd last been in my Curiosity Shop. He'd used the same set of gestures to plunge his hands playfully into my button boxes, stirring up their contents. But that wasn't all he'd been doing. Only now did I realise he must also have been palming the stolen netsuke bear in among the buttons. He was planting it on my premises in hope of incriminating me. Then he'd told Eden, who must have been frantic when he realised the bear was missing from the Japonisme display, that he'd seen it in my shop, expecting Eden to report it to the police, who would arrest me for dealing in stolen goods. So why didn't Eden do that?

Of course! Eden didn't want the theft to be public knowledge, because it would damage the museum's reputation for safe-guarding the treasures in their care – and his own, because as chief executive, the buck stopped with him.

So instead, he put Clive Thatcher on the case – poor, indebted gambler Clive, who would have done anything Eden asked in return for a bit of extra cash to help relieve his financial crisis (or, more likely, to fund another thrilling but doomed spree at the bookies).

Clive drew a blank posing as a button collector, but then the fair popped up, serving the precious bear netsuke to him on a plate – and with the comfort of a good disguise to keep the police off his scent.

Except Eden didn't trust Clive to return the bear to the museum, so took the extra precaution of being on hand to relieve Clive of it, all while keeping his distance from the person he was stealing it from. Eden must have thought he was Teflon-coated.

I practically ran round the rest of the door's revolution before allowing it to spill me out at the top of the steps that led down to the street.

I ran down the steps, taking them two at a time, until I reached the pavement. There I steadied myself by placing my hand on top of a handy pillar until I regained my composure. So that was the final riddle solved. Martin had stolen the wooden bear, intending to frame me as a thief or at the very least as a receiver of stolen goods.

So why hadn't Martin shopped me yet? He must have been biding his time. He knew I'd been involved in Broadwick's exhibi-tion of Japanese art a few years before, so he must have been expecting me to recognise the bear's value when I found it, and to put it up for sale either on eBay, where many lower-value and reproduction netsuke change hands, or, if I realised its true value, to send it to one of the big auction houses, such as Bonhams or Christie's. Either way, if Martin kept his eye on their websites as well as on eBay for new netsuke lots, he'd soon be able to catch me red-handed. Then he could get Norio Nagasaki to confirm the bear's identity and true value, and bring the sale to the attention of the police. In no time at all, he'd have me arrested for illegal trading practices.

At the same time, he'd no doubt score points with his boss, Adam Eden, who must have been in a frenzy of worry when he realised the bear had gone missing – stolen, I was sure, by Martin, who could have accessed its display cabinet using one of his many keys. The exhibition was due to end in February, when Eden would have to return the bear to its owner.

Checking my watch, I discovered I was overdue for my arrival at the Red Kimono. I set off along the Chipping at the fastest walking speed I could manage without looking absurd. Inside the restaurant, a pleasant young student type asked whether I had a reservation. When I told him I didn't, he said that although the booths were fully booked, there were plenty of spaces at the counter, and to take my pick of seats.

That couldn't have worked out better. I selected a high black stool with its back to the booth where Robert and Eden were already engaged in animated conversation. A tall, wide mirror at the centre of the conveyor belt gave me the perfect reflection of what they were up to, without my seeming to look at them. Whenever I gazed at the mirror to inspect them, I also played with my hair, to give the impression I was looking only at myself, experimenting with new hairstyles. Any diners watching me must have thought me terribly vain, but I didn't care.

I helped myself to a glass of water from the carafe on the

counter before sliding a pair of pale bamboo chopsticks out of their paper wrapper and rubbing them between my palms to separate them. Then I picked my first dish from the conveyor belt, a glistening purple bowl of rice stir-fried with slivers of chicken and vegetables. I quickly regretted my choice, as I needed to look at the dish while I was eating so as not to drop bits. Straining to hear Robert and Eden's conversation, I selected a more manageable green dish of edamame beans, glancing up at the mirror whenever I wasn't splitting the grass-green pods with my fingernails.

Fortunately, the jovial party in the booth adjoining Robert's chose to leave, and in the relative quiet of their departure I picked out more of his discussion with Eden.

When 'insurance' and 'brilliant broker' drifted across the gap between my seat and their booth, I guessed Robert had steered the conversation onto the tricky problem of negotiating and securing insurance cover for valuable loan items.

'I'm always pleased to receive recommendations of competitively priced services,' Eden was saying.

It didn't prove that a lack of insurance had been the reason Eden had been so secretive about recovering the missing exhibit, but his gratitude for Robert's recommendation certainly pointed that way.

'Special interest in Oriental art,' Robert was saying as I tucked into a pink bowl of neatly sculpted fresh fruit.

'My office in Singapore,' he dropped into the conversation, which would have added conviction.

Distracted by the arrival of a small, round sponge cake filled with custard and raspberry coulis now gliding past me, I stopped listening for a minute or two, waiting for the cake to come round again. I hoped no one else at the counter would nab it before it reached me. Snatching it up before it could pass by a second time, I set it on the counter in front of me. Before I could take a bite, my ears pricked up like an owl's to the rustling of a mouse in the undergrowth at the mention of a familiar name, not once, not twice, but three times.

'My country escape in Little Pride,' Robert was saying.

'Little Pride?' Adam almost shouted, dropping his chopsticks in his excitement, then his voice dropped to a whisper: 'Little Pride?'

The adrenaline now coursing through me must have boosted my sense of hearing, as I caught every syllable.

'I believe you know the village well?' Robert was saying casually. 'As does your IT manager Clive Thatcher, or should I say, your late IT manager. Weren't you worried how hard it would be to replace him?'

Wrong-footed, Eden tried to emulate Robert's cool manner.

'Oh, Clive Thatcher wasn't that irreplaceable. Personal problems, you know. He was bad with money. Last time he asked for a raise – which I didn't give him – he admitted to me he was fighting an online gambling habit. You'd think an IT manager would see through the empty promises of online betting campaigns, wouldn't you?'

This admission tipped Robert into a gamble of his own.

'And you'd think the CEO of an up-and-coming museum would take better care of its exhibits on loan and never let them leave its premises. But never mind, I have a small compensation for you. I think in your haste to leave Little Pride, you left this behind.'

In the mirror, I watched him pull from his pocket with the theatricality of a magician revealing a string of flags from his sleeve a familiar apple-green, hand-knitted scarf. Not the original one, I guessed, but a replica, that he must have had Mum secretly rustle up for the purpose. Clever!

Eden snapped, 'I don't know what you're talking about. You've no proof I've done anything wrong, and I resent your insinuations of my incompetence.'

I took this as my cue to join them. Robert, wide-eyed at my unscheduled interruption, budged along his bench seat to allow me to sit beside him.

'Oh, I think we do have proof, Mr Eden,' I began. 'You see, I happen to know your colleague Martin rather well, for reasons that need not concern you. And he has already confessed to me that he stole the netsuke bear and planted it in my shop, hoping to incriminate me for dealing in stolen goods.'

Robert gulped down some water. My blatant lie was clearly unnerving him, but I was convinced the risk was worth taking.

'But you didn't want to call the police, so you sent another loyal staffer to redeem it as surreptitiously as Martin had planted it. If only poor Clive had had the gumption to tell me what happened when he came to my shop posing as a button collector, rather than role-playing his idea of a secret agent, I'd have been prepared to sift through my button stock until he found it. But instead, he kept the truth to himself, and went on a completely unnecessary wild goose chase, causing unforgiveable havoc to my innocent friend Coralie.

'Then, having blown that opportunity, through online searches, he managed to establish where the bear now was: on a scarf knitted by my mum, going on sale at the Little Pride Christmas Fair.' I turned to Robert. 'The rest, I think we all know.'

Eden covered his face with his hands. 'Wretched Martin! I had a bad feeling about him when we employed him, but no, the rest of the board insisted that the vacancy needed to be filled as soon as possible, rather than to readvertise the post.'

'You don't deny it, then?' Robert said, unruffled.

Adam Eden stared at him, as if surprised to find he'd been voicing his thoughts aloud. Perhaps there were even more pressures building up in his job than we knew about.

Suddenly there was a crash as Eden leaped to his feet, overturning the sake carafe and his half-full glass. The waiter, sensing trouble – and perhaps keen to take extra care of what looked like potential strong tippers compared to the lone diners like me – rushed over to them, standing beside Eden to mop up the spillage with a linen napkin and by chance blocking his exit from the booth.

'Can I get you a fresh carafe, sir?' he said pleasantly.

Unable to escape the booth without physically shoving the waiter aside, Eden had apparently lost the power of speech.

'I don't think that will be necessary, thank you,' said Robert, unruffled as ever. 'I think we're just about done here. I'd be obliged if you could lock all the doors of the restaurant until the police arrive to take him away. Alice, you know what to do.'

I had my phone in my pocket at the ready, and I immediately dialled the emergency services. 'Police, please.'

'But I'm due back at my work by two,' cried a man in a high-street bank uniform at another booth.

'And me!'

'Me too!'

Robert stood up to address our fellow diners. 'Please allow me to pay for your lunches to make up for the inconvenience. And if your managers give you any grief about your late return, I'm sure our friend here' – he indicated the beaming waiter – 'will be glad to vouch for the valid reason you were detained.'

Eden had sunk into the corner of the booth, his complexion almost as red as the velvet on the padded bench seat.

'Now, how about a nice calming green tea while we wait for the police?' said Robert.

'Certainly, sir,' said the young waiter, signalling to one of his colleagues, who had to push past the chefs peering through the round windows in the kitchen doors to fulfil his order.

I jumped down from my seat and slid past the waiter to sit beside Eden, to create another obstacle on his exit route. When the second waiter brought our green tea, Robert and I raised a toast to each other.

45

THE CHRISTMAS PRESENT

I was glad the matter was over and done with well before Christmas Day, allowing us all to relax and start to anticipate what the new year might bring, rather than fretting about an unsolved murder mystery.

Both Adam Eden and Martin had been arrested, Eden on suspicion of murder, and Martin for theft and conspiracy. Neither were given bail.

Given the staff shortage this created at Highbere Museum, the trustees had rallied round to recruit replacements as quickly as possible. They'd been in touch with Danny to offer him a job after all. I was surprised that he didn't take it when earlier he'd seemed so keen, particularly now that Martin and Eden would no longer be there. I didn't find out why until Christmas morning, when Robert called round to collect me and Mum. His daughter, Belinda, had kindly invited us to join them for Christmas dinner at their elegant house in Great Pride. While I was trying not to read too much into her invitation, I was glad of the opportunity to spend this special occasion not only with Robert, but with dear little Tilly, a surrogate for the granddaughter I'd been unable to provide for Mum. I'd been getting closer to Belinda lately, too, and now counted her as a friend.

'Before we go, can I give you my Christmas present?' I asked Robert, dragging him by the hand to my Christmas tree, decorated by Mum in colourful knitted 'paper' chains, and topped with a pretty knitted angel all in white.

I'd already had a conversation with Belinda to agree Mum and I wouldn't be exchanging presents with her and her husband, and that we'd give Tilly only hand-knitted clothes as she already had so many toys. Wanting to give Robert his gift on my own turf, I pulled a bulky package out from under the tree and dropped it into his outstretched arms. He squeezed it with both hands.

'It feels like something soft and cuddly,' he said, before sitting down on the sofa to unwrap it.

As he held up the jumper to examine it, his face lit up.

'Did you make this yourself?' he asked, a note of hope in his voice.

I nodded.

'It's gorgeous. Nobody's knitted me a jumper since I was a little boy. That's really special. Thank you.'

I watched as he held it up against his chest to check the size. It looked like a perfect fit.

He set the jumper down on the coffee table and reached up to drag me down onto the sofa beside him. I didn't want to let him go.

But he drew back and pulled an envelope out of his inside jacket pocket, on which in his neat script – definitely his handwriting, and not some PA's – was written *To my darling Alice, Merry Christmas, with all my love.*

So, I guessed it was going to be a cheque or a gift voucher, or even just a few banknotes. That was disappointingly impersonal.

Oh well, I could treasure the envelope. At least his message had surpassed my expectations.

'Open it,' he urged, his eyes twinkling in anticipation.

I mentally prepared myself to thank him for however much or however little it was. What did wealthy people give each other for Christmas? I had no idea. I thought of the royal family, who famously always give each other cheap joke presents. I hoped this wasn't going to prove embarrassing.

It was nothing like that. What slid out of the envelope was a first-class plane ticket to Barbados, with a separate sheet confirming a five-star hotel had been booked for a week's stay. No, two plane tickets, and the hotel reservation was for a double room.

I glanced behind me, checking Mum was still out of earshot in the kitchen, before checking the name on the second ticket. I didn't want to embarrass myself by assuming Robert was inviting me to go on holiday with him, only to find he'd booked the trip for me and Mum.

Robert gave a nervous cough. 'I hope you don't think I'm being too presumptuous. I don't want it to seem like I'm taking you for granted. If you'd rather not go, I can get a refund. I just thought it would be good for us to get away together after all of the recent dramatics.' He looked a little sheepish. 'Now I think about it, this is as much a Christmas present to myself as to you. I'll buy you a nice souvenir while we're there, as a little extra.'

I flung my arms around him. 'Robert, that's the best Christmas present ever! But I don't think you'll need to pack your Christmas jumper.'

He laughed as he returned my hug, clearly relieved that I hadn't taken offence.

'Wait till I tell Danny!' I continued. 'He'll be so jealous.'

I sat back, and Robert reached for my hand, taking it in both of his. 'I don't think Danny will mind at all, actually. He'll still be too cock-a-hoop with his present to object.'

I tried not to let my face fall. 'You mean you're paying for him to join us?'

Much as I loved Danny, his presence would mean it wouldn't quite be the romantic idyll I'd hoped for.

'Good heavens, no! My gift to him is a new job. Starting as soon as possible.'

I knew Robert was kind, but I never expected such generosity.

'In the everlasting sponge business? That will be quite the career change.'

Robert chuckled. 'Oh, no. He's to be the founding curator of a new local museum.'

'Really? Where?'

Why hadn't Danny mentioned a new museum was opening up locally? Why hadn't I got wind of it from the local papers?

Robert let go of my hand and slipped his arm about my shoulders, pulling me closer to him. 'Do you remember me saying to him some time ago that a job with his name on it would turn up on his doorstep?'

I nodded.

'Actually, the new museum will be on his doorstep – or rather your doorstep. I've been saving this as a Christmas surprise, but the council has approved my planning application for the old paddock next to your cottage. My plan is to build a new local history museum there with the Roman mosaic we discovered there as its prime exhibit. I can't imagine a better person than Danny to run it, except you, of course, but you'll be too busy coping with the influx of visitors the new museum will bring your Curiosity Shop and café.'

For a moment, I couldn't find the words.

'That's fantastic!' I said at last. 'How very kind and generous you are, Robert.'

He smiled. 'It's not entirely unselfish, you know. I'm gaining a new business out of it.'

I didn't realise Mum had crept into the room until she spoke.

'Well, dear, if you ever need an extra pair of hands to help out in the shop once the museum's up and running, I'll always be pleased to come and stay.'

'Yes, Mum, that would be wonderful. Whenever and for however long you like.'

When I arose from the sofa to hug her too, Robert also got to his feet.

'Now, we'd better be on our way to Belinda's, or we'll have Tilly to answer to,' he said, clapping his hands together decisively.

'Yes, lovely Tilly,' said Mum.

For a moment I wished I was seven again, about to enjoy a family Christmas as a little girl with her and Dad. But then I looked at Robert, who was pulling his new jumper on over his taut chest, and realised that being fifty is not so bad after all.

* * *

MORE FROM DEBBIE YOUNG

The next cosy mystery from Debbie Young is available to order now here:

https://mybook.to/NewDebbieYoungBackAd

ACKNOWLEDGEMENTS

I've never seen a wool shop I didn't love, but this book is dedicated to the memory of the first wool shop I ever knew: Rema's, run by the kindly Mr and Mrs Kidd, in Sidcup, Kent, where I spent my childhood and my pocket money.

I grew up knitting – and loving button boxes – thanks to my lovely mum, who taught me to knit as soon as my hands were big enough to hold knitting needles. The first item I made was a yellow scarf for my dad. With unintentionally wavy edges, it was about two inches wide and eight inches long. My dad was over six feet tall. Despite its unsuitably small size, he accepted it graciously and putting it in his wardrobe, convincing me I'd mastered the craft. I've been an avid knitter ever since.

My earliest venture in sewing was much less successful. I was upset when my infant school teacher didn't appreciate the neat stitching on my first sewing card, just because I'd inadvertently sewed it to my skirt.

I'm thankful for the continuing inspiration supplied by the many ardent knitters in my life: as well as my mum, Grandma, Auntie Sheila, Auntie Thelma, my cousin Frances, my sister Mandy, my friend Elizabeth and her mum Gladys.

When I needed a name for Mrs Hardy's wool shop in this story, I asked my readers for ideas. Huge thanks to Emily Cotton, who was the first to suggest The Woolgatherer, my favourite out of many brilliant suggestions.

If this novel leaves you wanting to learn more about buttons and button boxes, I highly recommend Alan and Gillian Meredith's book, *Buttons*, a short but insightful guide for button collectors, and Lynn Knight's book, *The Button Box: Lifting the Lid on Women's Lives*, an intriguing women's history told through changing button fashions.

Finally, I must thank the wonderful team at my multi-award-winning publisher, Boldwood Books, for believing in Alice Carroll and helping me share her adventures with the world. Special thanks to Amanda Ridout, Rachel Faulkner-Willcocks, Becca Allen, Jacqueline Beard MBE, Claire Fenby, Marcela Torres, Jenna Houston, and Niamh Wallace, and to all those behind the scenes.

ABOUT THE AUTHOR

Debbie Young is the much-loved author of the Sophie Sayers and St Brides cosy crime mysteries. She lives in a Cotswold village, where she runs the local literary festival, and has worked at Westonbirt School, both of which provide inspiration for her writing.

Sign up to Debbie Young's mailing list for news, competitions and updates on future books.

Visit Debbie's Website: www.authordebbieyoung.com

Follow Debbie on social media:

X x.com/DebbieYoungBN
f facebook.com/AuthorDebbieYoung
BB bookbub.com/authors/debbie-young
O instagram.com/debbieyoungauthor

ALSO BY DEBBIE YOUNG

A Gemma Lamb Cozy Mystery

Dastardly Deeds at St Bride's

Sinister Stranger at St Bride's

Wicked Whispers at St Bride's

Artful Antics at St Bride's

A Sophie Sayers Cozy Mystery

Murder at the Vicarage

Best Murder in Show

Murder in the Manger

Murder at the Well

Springtime for Murder

Murder at the Mill

Murder Lost and Found

Murder in the Highlands

Driven to Murder

The Cotswold Curiosity Shop Mysteries

Death at the Old Curiosity Shop

Death at the Village Chess Club

Death at the Village Christmas Fair

POISON
& pens

POISON & PENS IS THE HOME OF
COZY MYSTERIES SO POUR YOURSELF
A CUP OF TEA & GET SLEUTHING!

DISCOVER PAGE-TURNING NOVELS FROM
YOUR FAVOURITE AUTHORS &
MEET NEW FRIENDS

JOIN OUR
FACEBOOK GROUP

BIT.LYPOISONANDPENSFB

SIGN UP TO OUR
NEWSLETTER

BIT.LY/POISONANDPENSNEWS

Boldw☾☾d

Boldwood Books is an award-winning fiction publishing company seeking out the best stories from around the world.

Find out more at www.boldwoodbooks.com

Join our reader community for brilliant books, competitions and offers!

Follow us
@BoldwoodBooks
@TheBoldBookClub

Sign up to our weekly deals newsletter

https://bit.ly/BoldwoodBNewsletter

Printed in Dunstable, United Kingdom